MW01123039

To

Audey AnGeemnen.

Famous Boy
Investigator Club

Rick and Joey Adventure Series

Written By:

Doris Taylor

Bloomington, IN Milton Keynes, UK

authorHOUSE™

Doris J Layler

9/17/06

AuthorHouse™
1663 Liberty Drive, Suite 200
Bloomington, IN 47403
www.authorhouse.com
Phone: 1-800-839-8640

AuthorHouse™ UK Ltd.
500 Avebury Boulevard
Central Milton Keynes, MK9 2BE
www.authorhouse.co.uk
Phone: 08001974150

© 2006 Doris Taylor. All rights reserved.

No part of this book may be reproduced, stored in a retrieval system, or transmitted by any means without the written permission of the author.

First published by AuthorHouse 5/8/2006

ISBN: 1-4259-2963-X (sc)

Library of Congress Control Number: 2006903090

Printed in the United States of America
Bloomington, Indiana

This book is printed on acid-free paper.

Cover Design by Khyri Taylor
Book Cover Illustrated by Laura E. Boice

My name is Khyri Taylor. I am 16 years old. I was born in Brooklyn, New York. I moved to Tarboro, North Carolina with my grandparents when I was younger. I watched my grandfather, Robert Taylor, draw and paint. He inspired me to learn how to draw, and I have continued to improve my drawing.

I am currently enrolled in Tarboro High School, where I am a junior. I've been taking art classes so I can become a better artist. My goals in life are to graduate from Tarboro High school, go to college and get a job using my art skills.

Contents

Dedication   ix

Acknowledgements   xi

Introduction   xiii

Chapter One   A PROBLEM TO SOLVE   1

Chapter Two   THE RESCUE   33

Chapter Three   THE TREE HOUSE   49

Chapter Four   MAKING PLANS   87

Chapter Five   A DAY AT THE CARNIVAL   117

Chapter Six   THE KIDNAPPING   138

Chapter Seven   THE ROBBERS   155

Chapter Eight   THE REWARD   178

Dedication

To my daughter, Robin Tolson,
for her ideas, encouragement, and support.

Acknowledgements

I would like to thank all of my friends who gave me so many ideas to write this book: Meade Horne who took time out of her busy schedule to help begin the editing process; George Adams, who volunteered to be the Chief of Police in the story; Chief Donnie Manning of the Tarboro Fire Department, who told me how to get Joey out of the tree; Justin Stewart, my fourteen-year-old reader for the blind, for sharing and reading many stories aloud to me; my editor, Terry Nelson Taylor, for her expertise, patience and understanding; and my grandson, Dillon Notz, who encourages me to write more adventure stories.

Introduction

This is the second book in the Rick and Joey Adventure Series. Rick and Joey Spencer are brothers with different ideas about how to approach life. Rick is very thoughtful, logical and organized in everything he does. However, Joey often acts without thinking and must face the consequences.

In the first book, *Rick and Joey's Great Adventure*, the brothers flew to their grandparent's farm for a summer vacation. Joey had many humorous encounters with the animals, and Rick's careful research lead to the discovery of a lost gold mine.

In this book, *The Famous Boy Investigators Club*, Rick enlists four of his friends to help stop a crime spree in their town of Mayfield, USA. Rick forms a club called the Famous Boy Investigator Club, or F.B.I. Club for short. Although Joey is too young to be a member, he always finds a way to get into the action. Soon the boys discover they are in need of a club house. They plan together to earn the money, and build their club house in a oak tree.

There are lots of surprises along the way and lots of hard work and challenges for these young boys from eleven to thirteen years of age.

Read and enjoy!!!.

chapter one

A PROBLEM TO SOLVE

Rick Spencer sat on the back porch of his home at 123 Spring Street, Mayfield, U.S.A. He was a studious-looking thirteen-year-old lad with the mind of a super-sleuth. His blond, curly hair framed his round face, and he wore gold wire-rimmed glasses. He was neatly dressed for a boy of his age, wearing tan cargo pants and a T-shirt with Indian Mountain painted on the front. He was deep in thought when he heard the phone ringing.

Mom said, "Rick, this phone call is for you," as she continued to prepare dinner.

"Coming, Mom," Rick replied. He took the cordless phone to the back porch. "Hello? Oh, hi! What's on your mind?" he said into the phone. Suddenly he became intently interested in the caller on the other end. "What?" he paused, listening to the caller. "Are you sure?" He paused again, drumming his fingers on the arm of the chair. "That might present a problem for the Famous Boy Investigators. Do you

1

have any ideas as to what we can do? Have you talked to your parents to see if it's true?" He paused again. "Let's call a meeting. Hold on! Let me ask my mom to see if we can meet here in my bedroom tonight. Will you call everybody? Let's plan it for seven o'clock, okay? Call me when you know how many boys can come. I should know by then if it's okay to have the meeting here. Thanks for calling." As he returned the phone to the kitchen, he noticed that his mom was busy, but he interrupted her. "Mom, can I have a meeting of the F.B.I. Club in my bedroom at seven o'clock tonight?"

"Is it really necessary?" Mom asked. "How many boys do you expect to meet in your bedroom?"

"Sam is doing the calling," Rick said. "He'll call me back and give me the answer as to how many boys plan to be here. Not to worry, Mom! We won't destroy my bedroom," he said with a smile.

"Can I come too?" Joey asked as he turned around and dried his hands on the towel that was tied around his waist, after washing a few dishes for his mother. "I want to be a Junior Investigator, too."

"Not this time, Joey," Rick replied. "You're not old enough to be a member. I told you before that you have to be eleven-and-a-half years old to join; besides, my bedroom isn't big enough for all of us."

"Rick, won't you reconsider letting Joey sit in on this meeting?" Mom inquired.

"But Mom, this meeting is important!" Rick said strongly. "We have a serious problem and we have to put our heads together to see if we can come up with a solution. After all, we are the Junior Investigators and solving problems is our mission," Rick replied, and his mom smiled at that remark.

"I'll talk it over with your dad," Mom replied. "I'll let you know in plenty of time to plan your meeting."

He returned to his chair on the back porch, sat with his right elbow on his knee and his palm resting against his chin. He was deep in thought about the conversation he had just had with his friend Sam.

Rick's dad, Detective Spencer, who had returned from work, came out the kitchen door and observed his son in deep concentration about a serious problem.

"Hi, son," Dad said. "Is something wrong?" He sat down on the chair next to Rick. He was wearing a blue blazer with his badge saying "Detective Richard Spencer" attached to the top of his pocket.

"Yes, Dad," Rick said sadly. "We boys of the F.B.I. Club have a problem. Sam Davis just called to let me know his parents are going to buy a new car and they want to park it in their garage. That means we can't meet there any more. Do you think you could help me solve this quandary?"

"That doesn't seem to be a problem," Dad replied, trying to figure out how he could help solve his son's dilemma. "You will just need to find another place to meet."

"It's not all that easy, Dad," Rick said, rubbing his brow as he put his thoughts in order. "It's like this: we need a new club house for our F.B.I. Club. We were meeting in Sam's garage, because he was the only one who had a place big enough for all our members."

"I asked Mom if we could have an emergency meeting in my bedroom tonight," Rick continued, "but Mom said she would get back to me after she talked to you first. I promise that we won't cause any trouble. What do you think?"-

"I understand your problem," Dad responded. "However, you need to check with your friends to see if they have someplace at any of their houses for your F.B.I. Club to meet. Meanwhile, I'll talk to your mother," he said, assuring his son that he agreed about the boys having a meeting. "How many boys do you expect?" he inquired.

"Gee, thanks, Dad," Rick said. "There will only be about five or six guys. Sam is calling all the members now, so when he returns my phone call, I'll know for sure how many plan to attend. This is such an important meeting, I'm so glad that you're in favor of it."

As Rick and Dad were continuing their conversation on the back porch, the phone rang. "That must be Sam. I'll be right back," Rick said as he headed into the kitchen. A few minutes later, Rick returned to the back porch.

"Was that Sam?" Dad inquired.

"Yes, Dad, it was," Rick answered. "He said there would be four more guys, so that would make five of us."

"It's fine with me," Dad said, heading into the kitchen. "I'll still need to check with your mother."

A few minutes later, Mom came to the kitchen door. "Rick, you can have your friends over tonight. Let them know that about six-thirty would be okay. Don't stay on the phone too long when you call Sam back, because dinner is almost ready."

"Thanks, Mom," Rick said, smiling, "This is such an important meeting."

Mom then walked into the living room. "Okay, boys, wash up, dinner is about ready," Mom instructed Dad and Joey.

"Oh, boy!" Joey exclaimed, jumping up from sitting on the floor, where he was playing with his PlayStation 2. "I'm sure hungry."

"I'm going over to see Uncle Gus after dinner," Dad said as he scooped some pot roast and vegetables onto his plate.

"That's nice, dear. I was planning on going shopping after dinner," Mom replied.

"That's fine," Dad responded. "I'll only be across the street. I need to check on Uncle Gus. I shouldn't be gone long. Do you boys think you can behave yourselves while we're out of the house for a couple of minutes?"

Joey jumped up. "Dad, Rick is going to have a meeting in his room; can I go, too?"

"Not this time, Joey," Rick said quickly as he passed the bowl of potatoes and pot roast to Joey. "I already told you that this is a serious meeting and we don't want any funny business."

"Joey, do you want to go with me to visit Uncle Gus?" Dad asked.

"No, Dad," Joey answered sadly. "I won't get into any trouble here at the house while you're away." He was still hoping Rick would change his mind.

At six-thirty that evening, Sam Davis and Pete Martinez knocked at the front door. Justin Stewart entered behind them.

"Dillon Notz called me to say he would be here by seven o'clock," Sam said as he walked past Rick. "He has to finish his chores before he leaves."

"Hi, Rick," Pete Martinez said as he passed Rick at the front door. He was short for eleven-and-a-half years old, with dark olive skin and large brown eyes. His straight black hair was cut to look like his mom had put a bowl on his head and cut all around it. He wore his Star Wars T-shirt and stone-washed jeans cut off just above his knees, with low-cut sneakers. Pete's mom referred to him as a "couch potato," but in reality he was a "computer spud." His mom encouraged him to get away from the computer games and go outdoors and exercise. Pete was not really overweight, but he was husky for his height. "Am I on time for the meeting?" Pete asked. "I have a lot of ideas to share with you guys."

Justin, who had just turned thirteen, had straight brown hair cut in a military style, and large brown eyes that complemented his complexion. He wore ragged cut-off jeans, a Sponge Bob Square Pants T-shirt, and white sneakers. "Hi, Rick," Justin said as he walked into the foyer. "I wasn't sure that I could make the meeting. My mother wasn't feeling well, so she said I could come if I would help with the dishes."

"Let's go upstairs to my room and we can wait on Dillon," Rick said, motioning his friends up the stairs.

"Can I come, too?" Joey asked, still hopeful.

"No, Joey, I told you NO," Rick said with authority. "I'll tell you what we've decided to do later. Now, go play and leave us alone!"

Rick closed his bedroom door so the Junior Investigators could get their ideas together.

"You just wait," Joey mumbled. "I'll get you for this." He stomped down the stairs. "I'll fix them." He stood in the kitchen letting the imagination of a younger brother run at full speed. "I got it!" he exclaimed to himself as he paced back and forth across the kitchen floor. "I'll make them let me into the meeting." He called to his mother and dad, but neither answered. "Oh yeah, Dad said he was going to Uncle Gus's and Mom is going shopping. I'll fix those boys if it's the last thing I do!" Joey opened the refrigerator door, found a bottle of ketchup, and poured it on his head, so it ran down his short, sandy blond hair onto his round face to the corner of his mouth. "I'll bet they will let me in the meeting now!" Joey said as he gingerly climbed the stairs and knocked on Rick's door. When Rick refused to open the door, Joey pushed it open, threw himself on the floor, and let out a blood-curdling scream.

"Holy Moley, what happened to Joey? He's bleeding to death! Let's call 911, Rick!" Sam said nervously, looking around for a phone.

"No, let's call my Dad," Rick said angrily as he ran to the window. "He's across the street with my Uncle Gus."

Justin Stewart knelt down beside Joey and asked, "How did you get hurt?"

Joey began giggling under his breath; he could hardly contain his laughter.

"He isn't hurt, guys, look, he's smiling," Justin said. "That's not even blood. It's just ketchup," Justin added, feeling the ooze between his fingers.

"Boy, are you going to get it!" Rick said sharply.

Joey began to burst out in laughter. "Can I come to the meeting now?"

"No, you can't," Rick replied as he opened the window and called to his Dad, who was sitting on the front porch with Uncle Gus. "Dad, please come home right away. Joey is in trouble again."

Detective Spencer hurried across the street and bounded up the stairs two at a time into Rick's room. To his surprise, when he entered the room, there on the floor lay Joey with red ooze covering most of his gooey, tousled blond hair and his face, and some on his white Atlas T-shirt.

"What happened here?" Detective Spencer asked as he looked down at his son lying on the floor. "Did you hurt yourself? Should I call for an ambulance?" Detective Spencer rushed to his son's side.

"No, Dad," Rick said sarcastically. "He doesn't need to go to the hospital, but he sure needs a good whipping. He is always causing trouble and we have some serious business to take care of. He just won't listen to me. This time he poured ketchup all over himself and interrupted our meeting, and who knows what he'll do next?"

It was seven o'clock, and there was a knock at the front door. Detective Spencer took Joey by the arm, led him down the stairs, and opened the door. It was Dillon Notz. "Go upstairs, Dillon, the guys are waiting for you."

"What happened to you?" Dillon asked snickering, seeing Joey covered with red ooze and his dad with an extra-firm hold on his arm. "You don't look so good, kid," Dillon remarked as he ascended the stairs.

When everyone had settled down, Rick took the roll call. "I'm calling this emergency meeting of the F.B.I. Club to order. I believe that Sam has told all of you why we're holding this emergency meeting. Sam's mother has bought a new car and is going to use their garage. We now need a new place to meet, a place of our own, where we can make plans for the Junior Investigators. Does anyone have any suggestions on where we can meet? "

"We can't meet at my house," Dillon spoke up first, "because my dad uses the garage and the other outbuilding to store his lawn equipment. He also has an office in the den, so that's out, too."

Dillon was tall for thirteen. He had light blond hair with bright blue eyes. He wore blue jeans, heavy work boots, and a green T-shirt with Jack and Jill Lawn Service printed on the back. You could see his developing muscles showing beneath the short-sleeved T-shirt.

"We can't meet at my house, because my mom is going to have a baby soon and she's already asking my sister and me to be quiet. If I had five or six boys over to my house, she would flip her lid," Pete replied.

"I would like to have the meeting at my house," Justin said, "but my grandmother is living with us and my mom is very busy taking care of her. My dad is an electrical engineer and he often works late in town. I know that my mom and dad wouldn't give me permission to have a bunch of guys over to my house."

"My dad is a contractor; and he works out of the house. He has every usable space taken up with his business stuff. He even uses the basement for his office," Sam said.

"I have an idea," Rick said. "I've been thinking about this all afternoon. I don't know if it will work, but it's worth investigating. I can ask my dad if we can build a tree house in our back yard, just like the one that Garth Waters used to have in his chestnut tree."

"You should wait until tomorrow to talk to your dad, Rick," Sam said. "I don't think he would be very agreeable right now. But I still think it's a great idea."

"I forgot about Garth's tree house. What happened to it?" Dillon asked.

"Don't you remember?" Justin remarked. "Garth's dad had most of those chestnut trees cut down because they caught some kind of disease."

"Yeah, I remember," Rick broke in. "The disease was called chestnut blight."

"That's right," Justin continued. "It's a contagious fungus that attacks only chestnut trees. That's why Garth's dad had to have all of the sick trees cut down. The logs were hauled to the sawmill for lumber."

"The tree with the house in it wasn't cut down," Sam continued the story, "because it didn't have the disease, but last September Hurricane Hilda uprooted it and demolished the tree house."

"Sure," Pete answered. "My Uncle Charlie cut down those chestnut trees and took the logs to the sawmill. Remember Hurricane Hilda? Well, my Uncle Charlie told Mr. Waters that if he cut down all of the chestnut trees except one, and a strong wind came in from the

Northeast, there would be a chance it would blow the tree over. Mr. Waters wouldn't listen to good advice. After Hurricane Hilda, the last tree with the tree house was on the ground."

"I have a suggestion," Justin said. "Since we are investigators, I think we should investigate our options. Surely we can find a place to meet. What do you think?"

"That's a wonderful suggestion," Rick said, taking his cap on and off while combing his fingers through his blond hair. "Okay! Sam, would you get on the Internet and find out all about club houses, tree houses, and any other way to hold a meeting that doesn't take up too much room and doesn't cost an arm and a leg?"

"I'll be glad to do that," Sam said. "I'll print out all the info I can find. Then we can discuss it at our next meeting."

Pete spoke up. "Can Justin and I go over to Garth Waters' house and ask him how much it cost to build his tree house, how big it was, and how many sleeping bags could fit on the floor?"

"I'll be glad to go," Justin Stewart added. "I'd like to have a tree house in my back yard, but we're just renting and my mom and dad would say no."

"I'll go to the library and look up as much information as I can find about tree houses," Rick said. "Let's have another meeting on Saturday afternoon at one-thirty in the park, so we can discuss what we have found out."

"Let's adjourn the meeting and everyone do their investigations. We might find something that would work for our club house," Rick concluded.

The boys hurried home to consider their challenges.

*****

After a big Saturday breakfast, Rick and his dad sat on the back porch. Rick gathered all his nerve and asked, "Can we build a club house here in our back yard?"

"We don't have any room to build a club house here, son." Dad replied, as he looked over the tiny back yard with an old oak tree taking up most of the space.

"Sure we do," Rick said, "Don't you remember the tree house that Garth Waters had? It was built in an old spreading chestnut tree in his back yard. It was really neat, but when Hilda, that last hurricane, came through, it blew the tree over and the tree house was destroyed. His dad said that since the blight hit most of their trees, it was better to have them cut down so the blight would not hurt the other chestnut trees in the neighborhood."

"What is Chestnut Blight?" Dad asked. "I know I have heard of it, but I didn't know that it was contagious."

"The blight is a fungus disease that rots the tree from the inside out. This left the tree house with no protection. That's what Garth told me, anyway. "

"Well, how do you plan to build a club house in this old oak tree in our back yard?" Dad asked. "Do you know that another hurricane could come through and destroy your new tree house, too?"

"I suppose so," Rick replied, "but Pete's Uncle Charlie said that with our oak tree being so close to the house, it would be protected from the wind and even hurricanes. Each of our club members was given a job investigating the options. Sam was to research tree houses on the Internet. I went to the library to research tree houses, too," Rick related, and Pete and Justin went over to Garth's house to get info from him, both the good and the bad things, about his tree house."

"What did you find out?" Dad asked.

"I found out that it would cost ten dollars to get a copy of the plans to build a tree house. That seemed too expensive for me," Rick said. "We have a meeting planned at the park this afternoon. We will discuss all of our options, and I'll let you know what we decide. Okay?" Rick replied to his dad.

"Thanks, son," Dad replied. "I'll be anxious to hear about your progress. Good luck in your search for a new meeting place."

At one-thirty, Rick, Joey, Sam, Justin, and Dillon rode their bikes to the park. When they arrived, the first shelter at the entrance was vacant. "This looks like a good place to meet," Rick said. So the boys gathered around the large cement picnic table inside to discuss their options.

Rick called the meeting to order. "Did everyone have enough time to complete the investigations they were assigned to do?" Rick asked.

The boys nodded, and a chorus of "Yeah! Ready! I'm done!" was echoed by everyone.

"Justin, what did you find out at Garth Waters' house?" Rick asked, taking his notebook from his pocket.

"When Pete and I got to Garth's house," Justin related, "he took us up to his room where he showed us some pictures. I spotted a picture, blown up into a large poster, of his tree house that hung on the wall over his bed. It had two windows, one on each side of the door. It had a wooden ladder nailed to the little porch at the entrance. The large leaves on the chestnut tree hid a lot of the tree house. He said he and his scoutmaster built the tree house at the base of the four large limbs of the tree. Then he went to the storage shelf of his headboard and took out a packet of photos that he had taken of the inside of the tree house. They were neat. The photos were filled with ideas that we could use in our tree house. The tree house had benches around the back wall that opened to hold the sleeping bags, dishes and other supplies. They were like window seats. He used the tree house for Scout meetings and sleepovers with his Boy Scout troop. He said that it cost about two hundred and fifty dollars because most of the lumber was donated. The other money was earned by selling magazines and many bake sales they had outside the mall. With the loss of the tree house, they now have to meet in the basement of St. James Methodist Church. We even saw his Boy Scout sash with all of his patches on it hanging from his corkboard. He must really be into Scouting. There were five Scouts plus the troop leader. He showed us a picture of how the sleeping bags were laid out. Later, Garth's dad came up to the room. He told us that the biggest mistake he made was to cut down the entire grove instead of only the diseased chestnut trees. Garth's tree was left standing alone without protection. Then when Hurricane Hilda came along, the tree was uprooted and fell to the ground, and the tree house was destroyed."

"We invited Garth to join our F.B.I. Club and help us build our tree house in the oak tree in Rick Spencer's back yard," Pete said.

"Garth said he would talk it over with his dad and then decide if he wants to help us," Justin related. "I told him that if he decided to join us, to please bring the pictures to our meeting at one-thirty this afternoon. I told him we were going to meet at the park. Do you think it's okay, Rick?"

"Yes," Rick replied. "That was a very good idea to invite him to the meeting. First of all, he would get to know the other members. Then he would know for sure that we're a fine group of boys."

"I told Garth that since he had already built a tree house," Pete related, "why not join the F.B.I. Club? He had the experience, and I thought Rick and the other members would be glad to have him join us. What do you think?"

"Good show, Pete," Rick said. "We sure need a person with his experience to be a member of our club."

"Garth and his dad asked me," Justin continued, "what is the F.B.I Club anyway? They'd never heard of it before. I told them that it's the abbreviation for the Famous Boy Investigators Club, and that we help the police solve crimes. I told them about how we ride our bikes around the neighborhoods at night to see if anything looks suspicious and sometimes we call the police."

Just then, Garth Waters rode up to the park entrance on his bike. He stopped and spotted the club members sitting at the shelter. "Hi guys," Garth said. "I decided to join your club. My dad said that I could as long as it didn't interfere with my Scout meetings. Did you know I plan on being an Eagle Scout before I graduate high school? I have most of my badges. I have fulfilled all of my requirements for Star and Life achievements and some of the requirements for my Eagle rank. I also enjoy building things."

"Welcome aboard," Rick said to Garth, as he shook his hand. "I hope you will give us some of your expertise on how to build a tree house. Did you bring the pictures of your tree house?"

"Yes, I did," Garth said, as he passed the pictures around to the members who were sitting at the picnic table.

"Can I keep the pictures for future reference?" Rick asked.

"Sure you can," Garth responded proudly. "These are copies; I left the negatives at home. You can keep these."

"Thanks," Rick said. "We're keeping a scrapbook of all our activities. Sam, how did you do with your research?"

"I did pretty well," Sam replied. "I searched on the Internet and found several sets of plans for constructing a tree house. I downloaded two sets of plans and checked the prices of the materials. It looks like the Mayfield Lumber Yard has the best prices, if we decide to use new wood. Maybe somebody will donate some used lumber for our tree house. One set of plans is for a "Classic" style of tree house. It seems to be the easiest to construct. The other plan is called the "Cabin" style. It appears to be too complicated for us to build. I didn't find any other plans that suited our needs."

"Yesterday I went to the library," Rick reported. "I looked up information on tree houses in many magazines and found several good pictures. But, they wanted ten dollars for a copy of the plans. I felt that was too expensive for our club. So, I just wrote down the list of materials to get a better idea of what it would take to construct a tree house. I'm glad that you got the better information, Sam. Now that Garth is going to help, it should be a piece of cake!"

"Does anyone have any other ideas before we put the plans up for a vote?" Rick concluded.

"Yes, I do," Sam replied. "The first order of business should be that we decide on how we're going to raise the money to build this tree house."

"My mom said she would give us some money," Pete said. "She was so happy when I told her about this tree house. She is very glad that I'll be away from the computer and playing out in the fresh air."

"That's one way to get the money," Dillon said. "I could ask my parents for money, too. But, it would be better if we raised our own funds. Then we're not obligated to anyone."

"My Uncle Charlie said that he will give us some help, too," Pete said. "He's a construction engineer and knows how to build houses, so maybe he can help us build a tree house."

"I suggest that we gather empty aluminum cans from the trash barrels in the park and anywhere else we can find them. We can take them to the recycling center for cash," Justin said.

"There's a house under construction over on Maple Drive," Garth reported. "We can ask the foreman if we can work cleaning up the job site. He would probably pay us cash."

"We can put up signs in the supermarket advertising that we will do odd jobs, even clean out garages," Sam said, wrinkling his nose. He was thinking about how hard the work could be.

"There's also a house under construction over on Elm Drive," Justin said. "I know the foreman over there. Let me ask him if we could work to clean up the job site. I'll bet he'd pay us to pick up and stack the lumber and pick up the trash, too."

"That sounds like a good option to me," Rick said. "Who wants to go over and ask the foreman on Elm Drive tomorrow morning? Then we can go over and see the foreman on Maple Drive while we're at it. Are there any more suggestions?"

"I'll go with you." Sam replied quickly.

"Okay," Rick said. "Thanks, Sam." Then he continued, "Okay, this will be Item Number One for this meeting. Any further discussion on Item Number One?"

When no one replied, Rick continued, "Now let's put these ideas to a vote. Item Number One..."

Justin interrupted, "Hey, aren't we going to have a secret vote?"

"No, we will try to use Parliamentary Procedure," said Rick. "Didn't you pay attention in sixth grade Social Studies class? You can hold your hand up to vote for or vote against. That's how we do it!"

"Item Number One, again," Rick said with a slightly frustrated look on his face. "We have two sets of plans for tree houses. Has everyone had a chance to look over each set of plans? One is the 'Classic style,' which looks easy to construct." The boys all nodded yes. "The other plan is the 'Cabin style.' It's pretty fancy. Also, it looks like it would be too complicated for us to build. So let's vote on the 'Classic' for

Item Number One. All those in favor of building the Classic style tree house raise your right hands, and I will count the votes. I see five votes in favor and no votes against. Motion passed." After a pause, and not hearing any discussion, he stated, "It is agreed that we will build the 'Classic.'"

"Item Number Two," he continued, "would be gathering empty aluminum cans. Is there any discussion?"

Dillon stood up, "I heard the price of aluminum is high right now. If we work hard picking up empty aluminum cans, we should be able to raise a good sum of cash," he stated.

"Is there any further discussion on Item Number Two?" Rick asked. Not hearing any, he continued, "All those in favor of collecting aluminum cans for recycling hold up your right hands high so I can see them. I will now count the votes. That's five in favor, none against. Motion carried."

"Item Number Three," he went on. "Garth and Justin suggested that we ask the foremen of the construction sites on Maple and Elm Drives if we can work to clean up the sites in exchange for materials or cash. All in favor of working at the construction sites hold up your hands. It looks like four votes in favor. Are there any votes against working at the job sites? One. Motion carried."

"I want you to notice that I voted against cleaning up the construction sites," Joey said. "I don't want to work picking up nails and do dumb stuff like that. That's too much work for me. There are two job sites to clean, and I don't want to be a part of that!"

Joey crossed his arms and stomped.

"Okay Joey, you're not even a member," said Rick, remembering the ketchup incident. "You don't have to do it. Please come back and sit down and be quiet until the meeting is over."

"Okay," Rick continued. "Is there anybody else who wants to back out of cleaning up the construction sites?" He hoped that Joey's behavior would not cause another boy to change his mind.

Pete stood up and said, "I don't want to do it either. I just thought about it, and I remembered that I stepped on a nail last summer and I don't want to do it again. Count me against."

"Okay," Rick said. "Does anyone else want to back out of cleaning up the construction sites?" Not hearing anybody else decline to work at the construction sites, Rick continued.

"All right, Pete. You don't have to do it either." Rick marked Pete and Joey's names off of the construction site list.

"Item Number Four: making posters and flyers for advertising. Is there any discussion?"

I don't know what to write," Pete said, "and we'd need someone to hand out the flyers."

"I'll hand out the flyers in front of the mall on Saturday afternoon," Joey said, trying to act like he was a member.

Sam said, wrinkling his nose, "I don't want to make posters." Several of the boys grumbled.

"All those in favor of advertising for odd jobs by making posters and flyers, also putting up the posters in the supermarket and handing out the flyers, raise your hands. I see only two votes in favor. Are there any no votes? There are four votes against it. Motion failed," Rick said. "Good try anyway, guys.

"Item Number Five is to ask our parents for money to help pay for the tree house. Is there any discussion?"

"Yes," Justin spoke up. "I don't think we should ask our parents for the money. We need to do this job on our own. What do you think?"

The agreement was echoed among the boys. Garth said, "Let's let our parents know that we are responsible enough to earn the money to build the tree house by ourselves."

"I agree," Sam replied. "I'm ready to vote. Let's vote on Item Number Five."

Rick continued with the final vote, "All those in favor of asking our parents for the cash to build the tree house, raise your hand. I count two votes in favor and four votes against. Motion failed."

Everybody shouted in unison, "We'll do it ourselves!" With nothing further to vote on, Rick closed that portion of the meeting.

"Does anybody have any more news to report?" Rick asked. Not hearing any, Rick continued, "Sam and anybody else who wants to go with me to meet the foremen Monday morning, be at my house at eight o'clock. Then we can go over and meet the foreman at each job site together. You can come too, Pete. Since you don't want to work on the construction sites, I will put you in charge of collecting the aluminum cans. The rest of us will meet with the foremen on the construction sites. Let's adjourn this meeting and go home for supper. Thanks for coming to the meeting. I think we all did a good job investigating our options," Rick said. "Everyone is invited to my house for a cookout. My dad bought a new grill and loves to barbecue. It might just be hamburgers and hot dogs, but it will be supper for us."

When the boys arrived at Rick's house, Mr. Spencer was mowing the grass in the back yard. "You boys are just in time to help me rake the grass and bag it," Mr. Spencer said. "By the way, how did your meeting go?"

"It went very well," Pete said. "Justin and I went over to visit Garth Waters. He has decided to become a member of our club. He will help us since he has experience, because he built his own tree house. He is also going to help us gather soda cans for recycling. With all of us boys working together, we should have the money to build the tree house in no time at all."

Dad replied, "That could be true, but if you do get the money, how do you expect to build this tree house?"

"Well, first of all, we have detailed plans, Rick answered. "I asked Uncle Gus to come over and check the tree out for sturdiness. Maybe he can help us throughout the construction of the tree house. He can at least give us suggestions when we get stuck and need advice."

"By the way," said Dad with a smile, "do you know how much it is going to cost to build the tree house? Do you think you can earn enough money recycling, and cleaning up the construction sites?"

"Yes, we have a pretty good idea," Rick said. "The materials are going to cost about five hundred dollars. With the six of us working on this project, we should earn the money quickly. If you have a couple of minutes, Dad, we can go to the back porch and I'll show you what information I have."

Mr. Spencer turned off the mower. He and Rick went to the back porch while the others gathered the grass trimmings.

"Dad, here are the calculations and the list of materials. Sam got these from Mayfield Lumber Yard and the One Stop Hardware Store. It looks like Mayfield has the best prices for new wood. They told us it would cost five hundred dollars for all the materials and supplies. One Stop Hardware specializes in used lumber, but we feel that new lumber is best."

"We all agreed on recycling aluminum cans. Dillon found out that the recycling center is paying fifty-five cents a pound for aluminum. When we finish picking up the grass trimmings, would you give us some of your trash bags for our cans?" Rick asked.

"Sure thing, Son," Dad responded. "You can have as many bags you want."

The boys arrived at the back porch after helping to collect all the grass cuttings. "But don't leave now. Aren't you boys going to stay for the cookout?" Dad inquired.

"Sure, we're all looking forward to it!" Dillon said, smacking his lips. The other boys yelled, "We're hungry! Where's the beef?"

"Here, Dad, are the plans we voted on. Do you want to look at them? You can give us some advice to get started," Rick said, smiling.

"Yes, I do," Dad replied, as he scanned the many pages of the plans. "I'll look them over and let you know what I think," he said.

"Thanks, Dad," Rick said. "I hope you can help us get organized."

"I'd be glad to help you get organized," Dad said, "but you know that Uncle Gus is a contractor. Maybe he could give you better information as to the cost and the materials needed. You sure did a thorough research job on this project," Dad remarked. "Someday, you'll make a great detective."

"That's my goal," Rick replied proudly. "I want to be as good a detective as you are, and there's no time like the present to begin."

"Thanks for the compliment, son! I'm proud of you and your friends, but gathering empty aluminum cans won't bring in enough money quickly," Dad said thoughtfully.

"We are going to ask the foremen if we can work cleaning up the job sites in exchange for some of the materials on our list. They might even pay us something for doing the work. We feel that we can have the tree house built in a few weeks," Rick said.

"By the way, how did you manage to get elected head of this project?" Dad asked.

"I was voted President of the F.B.I. Club and Sam was voted Vice-President, because we both like to research information. We were the best qualified among the Junior Investigators," Rick said with pride. "Sam also helped with the research."

"Can you explain to me what the F.B.I. Club really is?" Dad asked.

"The F.B.I. means the Famous Boy Investigators Club," Rick replied, almost boasting. "Don't you remember how our group of boys helped the police find shoplifters and gangs of boys breaking windows over at the elementary school last summer?"

"Oh yes, I remember," Dad said, "but it wasn't known as the F.B.I. Club then, was it?"

"No, I guess it wasn't. We just couldn't get organized. But last month, I asked another group of boys if they were serious about investigating crimes and helping the police, and this time, I only took those who were serious," Rick said. "My friends from last summer only wanted to play."

Dad continued, "I want to remind you that you were in a very dangerous situation for you boys to get involved with. Nowadays there are a lot of killings with no thought for human life. I wish you boys could find other ways to do public service."

"We promise to use safety first, Dad," Rick said. "Last summer, we didn't have enough boys to make a club. When we returned to school this fall, I made a lot of new friends. I have asked several boys to join the F.B.I. Club. Now we have ten members, but only seven of us are really active in the club."

Dad said sympathetically, "That's usually how it works. Some just want their name on the membership, but they're too busy to get their hands dirty. Let me study these plans and I'll give the old oak tree a once-over."

"I asked my Uncle Charlie," Pete added. "He said he would give us some advice, but he wanted us to build it ourselves."

After the cookout, Rick told the boys, "My dad and I reviewed the decisions we made at the F.B.I. meeting this afternoon."

Sam asked, "What did your dad have to say?"

Dillon interrupted. "Did he like our plans to build the Classic style tree house?"

"Yes, he is very much in favor of us building the Classic style tree house. I was surprised because he wasn't sure it could be done. He was concerned about us earning enough money to complete the project, but I convinced him that we are all going to work hard to finish the tree house."

"Hip! Hip! Hurray! Three cheers for Rick. You did a great job for us," Pete said.

"In the meantime," Rick said, "Pete, you can start collecting empty aluminum cans. Why not start asking the neighbors if they have any and if they will save them for us? When we get enough, we're going to take them to the recycling center. This will give us a little cash to begin building our tree house. Now let's get busy and start finding cans."

"That would be a big help to the F.B.I. Club," Sam replied. "This will help us reach our goal in no time at all."

"Thanks for the cookout, Mr. Spencer," each boy said as they mounted their bikes and rode home.

Later that evening, when Rick was preparing to go to bed, Dad entered his room. "Come to think of it, son, I might be able to help you after all," Dad said. "Before you go to sleep, I have an idea to share with you. I go bowling every Friday evening. I can ask the owner of the bowling alley if he will save the soda cans for me. I've seen several barrels full of empty cans. I don't know if he takes them to the recycling center, but I can ask."

"That would be helpful to the F.B.I. Club," Rick said, yawning as he slipped into bed. "Thanks a lot, Dad."

*****

Early Monday morning, Sam Davis and Pete Martinez rode their bikes into Rick's back yard, ready to meet Rick and head to the construction sites.

Sam was thirteen. He had lots of curly brown hair that he stuffed under a baseball cap he wore backwards. He was tall with brawny muscles that showed beneath his blue knit tank top. He wore khaki cargo shorts and high-top sneakers.

Pete was eleven-and-a-half years old. He was wearing a baseball shirt with number 48 on the back, white shorts and baseball shoes. He had his high-top sneakers tied to the handlebars of his bike, just in case he needed them.

"We brought some heavy trash bags to gather up more aluminum cans," Sam said as he and Pete dismounted their bikes.

"My brother Tom said he would meet us at the entrance to the park at four o'clock this afternoon," Pete said. "He will drive us to the recycling center. Also he will tell us if the work we put into gathering cans was worthwhile."

As the boys were preparing to leave, Rick's dad stopped them. He reminded the boys, "Just remember, safety first."

"Sure thing," Rick replied. "We all will be careful. Dad, is it okay for us to head out to the job site? First, Sam and

I are going to head down to the construction site on Maple Drive. I spoke to Mr. Smith, the foreman, yesterday. He said we could clean up the construction site whenever we have the time. He is going to pay each of us twenty dollars a day. Next, we need to begin our investigative work and see how much money we can earn today," Rick said. "Joey doesn't want to work on the construction site, so I think we should leave him at home."

"Now, Rick," Dad answered, "be nice to your brother and let him help. One day Joey will be a member of the club, and the tree house is in his yard, too."

"Aw, Dad," Rick pleaded, "you know how much trouble he gets into. Isn't there any other way for him to help from home?"

"I had a long discussion with him after the ketchup incident," Dad replied. "Joey promised to listen to you from now on."

"Well, maybe that will be okay. We're one member short anyway. Dillon won't be able to help us very often with our project. He has lawn work to do and I don't think his dad will let him take the time off to gather soda cans during the week," Rick said. He paused for a long moment, thinking the problem over in his mind. "I guess Joey can go with Pete and gather cans."

"That's the spirit, Rick," Dad said with a smile. "I'll call him for you. He's been helping your mother in the kitchen.

By the way, you had better take some work gloves with you. Who knows what else is in those trash baskets!"

"Okay," Rick replied. "We need those large canvas laundry bags too. They should hold a lot of cans."

"I reviewed your plans, son, and found that the set called "Classic" is easiest to build," Dad responded encouragingly.

While the boys were examining the plans for the tree house, Garth rode his bike at high speed into the driveway. "Sorry to be late," he said. "I had to finish mowing Mrs. King's lawn."

"Has anybody seen Joey lately?" Dad asked. "He isn't in the kitchen."

"Joey isn't here, Dad," Rick said. "He told me he was going over to see Uncle Gus to ask him to help us build the tree house. He should be back shortly."

chapter two

THE RESCUE

A short time later, Joey and Rick came out the back door, each carrying a large canvas laundry bag. Joey had on his favorite T-shirt. The stain left from the ketchup episode was clearly visible. His Atlas cap covered his short, curly, blond hair. He was wearing new white cargo pants. A Swiss Army penknife was in one of the pockets, an instant camera in another. In fact, all of his pockets seemed to be crammed full of his favorite trinkets.

"Joey, why do you have so much stuff in all of your pockets?" Rick asked. "You won't be able to bend over to pick up any cans."

"It's okay, Rick," Joey said bravely. "I'll be able to bend over. My pants will get looser as I ride my bike."

Rick said, "All right Joey, I'm not going to argue with you. Listen up! Dillon Notz called me on the phone. He'll meet us at the park as soon as possible. First, Sam and I are going over to work on the construction site. Then we'll meet you at the park as soon as we finish."

Pete, Garth, and Joey mounted their bikes and headed to the park. They rode their bikes around the paved paths, stopping at each trash basket to fill their bags for the recycling project. Pete and Garth also rode to the picnic shelters in their search. Soon two of the trash bags were filled to the brim with crushed aluminum cans.

Later in the morning, Rick and Sam returned from the construction site to join in the search for empty cans.

"Where's Joey?" Rick asked, not seeing him and hoping he wasn't in trouble again.

"The last time we saw him, he was riding towards the boat ramp," Garth said. "Maybe he's still there. Do you want to ride over and check?"

"Yes," Rick said, "I think we should check on him. Who knows what he's up to?"

"We may as well ride over there anyway," Garth said. "I think we got all of the empty cans from this side of the lake. Let's check out the other side of the lake and see if there are any cans over there."

As the boys rode toward the boat ramp, Joey called out. "Hey guys, wait for me. I was just on my way up to the picnic area. I rode to the boat ramp. There were plenty of empty cans there. I think I got them all," Joey said as he showed the boys his haul.

Pete told Rick that as he and Garth rode from trash can to trash can, they saw posters of a lost dog. The picture showed a yellow, curly-haired Cocker Spaniel, with floppy ears so long that they reached his chin. "Printed below the picture was his name—'Speed Bump'—and a $25.00 reward for the rescue and return of the lost dog," Garth said.

"Wow! A $25.00 reward! We can really use the money. What do the rest of you guys think?" Pete asked enthusiastically.

"Let's get our investigation going now!" Sam shouted. "The $25.00 reward will pay for a lot of the materials for the tree house."

Seeing a group of boys fishing at the edge of the lake, Sam called to them, "Hey, guys! Did anyone see a dog running around without a leash?"

"No! We haven't seen a lost dog," the boys yelled back to Sam.

Pete cupped his hands around his eyes so he looked like he had a pair of binoculars. He scanned the area around the lake where they were standing. "No, I don't see any lost dogs," Pete remarked to Sam. "Let's ride over the bridge to the other side of the lake. Cocker Spaniels like to run and splash in the water. I'll bet the missing dog is down there playing at the water's edge."

"Yeah," Garth said, "the trees are thicker and it's probably cooler on the other side, too."

"Okay," Rick said as he checked his watch. "It's one-thirty, so we have about an hour to try to find the dog. We told mom we would be home by two thirty. If we don't find the dog today, we can always come back tomorrow."

Pete and Joey held their bags of cans high on their handlebars, so they would not get caught in the wheels or pedals of their bikes. Garth held his full bag of crushed cans over his shoulder with one hand and steered his bike with the other hand.

When they reached the other side of the lake, they rode close to the shoreline looking for the dog.

"Hey, guys," Pete said, "I see a thick cypress grove over there on the left side of the shore. Let's ride over there and investigate."

"We've looked everywhere else. Maybe we'll hit pay dirt this time," Sam said. As they approached the cypress grove, they heard a whimpering cry. The boys stopped and listened intently, and they heard the cry again. They jumped off their bikes and ran to the edge of the water, all except for Joey, who was taking pictures while riding his bike in the opposite direction. Rick and Sam looked through the cypress trees that lined the shore. At the water's edge there were large cypress "knees" that are the cypress roots. They looked like round bald-headed gnomes, poking out of the water. These round roots gave a mysterious look to the shady marshland. The saw grass was waving near the top of the water. They followed the sad, fearful cry until they came to the marshy area. Finally, they found what they were seeking. The shivering yellow Cocker Spaniel pup looked like he was tangled up in some weeds. He cried in a sorrowful yelp, letting the boys know that he was in trouble and very, very tired.

"Look! I see the lost dog! It looks like he's stuck on something. I'll go in after him," Sam said courageously. "I know how to swim. I can save him. I don't think he would bite. This pup only wants to get out of the tangled mess he's in."

"Wait a second, Sam. I have an idea. You can use the string from my laundry bag," Rick said. "Take this cord with you. Try to tie it onto his collar. Then maybe you can pull him out of the water."

Sam took the strong cord from Rick and waded out into the lake. His tennis shoes were being sucked into the marshy mud. He struggled with each step, but he continued wading until he reached the stranded dog.

"Good boy, I'm not going to hurt you," Sam said as he patted the stranded pup on his head, reassuring the pup that he would be saved. Then Sam ran his hands under the dog. He found that he was stuck in twisted fishing line and tangled marsh grass. "Does anyone have a pen knife or something I can use to cut him loose?" he called back to shore.

"I have my Swiss Army penknife in my pocket," Joey volunteered. He dropped his bike quickly on the ground and removed all the items from his new white cargo pants except his Swiss Army penknife. Then Joey waded into the murky lake water before the other boys could stop him. Suddenly, his feet slipped off the slippery ledge of the lake and he slid under the water. He hadn't realized how slippery the bottom of the lake was. Joey did not come back up right away.

"Don't let him drown, Sam!" Rick yelled. "My mom and dad will never forgive me!" Rick could feel his heart pounding. What would he do without his brother? Rick prayed silently, "Dear God, don't let anything bad happen to my brother Joey."

Sam left the stranded pup and waded over to where Joey had disappeared under the water. He felt all around for Joey. The water was muddy and deep. It was over Sam's shoulders. He dove under the water and couldn't see anything because the water was so muddy. He splashed as he rose to the surface to get another breath of air and went under again. Finally, he bumped into Joey. Sam grabbed Joey's arm and pulled him to the surface. "Come on, Joey!" Sam squeezed Joey's chest, and murky water came out of Joey's mouth. "Are you all right?"

"I think so," Joey said, and threw up lake water all over himself.

Sam called back to shore, "He's okay, he didn't drown. Rick come and help me get him back to shore. He's full of lake water!

Joey spit and sputtered. "I'm sorry!" he gurgled weakly. "I only wanted to help."

"But you had better have that penknife, boy!" Sam said harshly, as he kept Joey's head out of the water.

Still waterlogged and slightly shaken, Joey handed Sam his red Swiss Army penknife. "I'm sorry to cause so much trouble, I just wanted to help," Joey choked.

Rick waded into the lake to retrieve his brother, who was still coughing and spitting up the murky, green lake water.

"That wasn't a smart thing to do, Joey. You should have given Sam the penknife before he went in the water," Rick scolded. "Couldn't you see that he needed it to cut the weeds away?"

"No," Joey responded. "I really didn't see what was going on because I was busy taking pictures, but I came right away when I heard Sam say he needed a penknife."

Rick pulled Joey to shore, laid him face-down on the ground, and tried to dry him off. He pressed Joey's back to force the water out of his lungs and stomach. "Boy, you have to stay out of trouble or you will have to stay home with Mom and Dad," Rick said. "Oh my, wait until Mom sees your new white pants. She will have a fit!" Rick scraped the mud and weeds from Joey's clothes as best he could.

With Joey safely out of the water, Sam returned to rescue the lost pup. Sam put the penknife between his teeth. He used both hands to move the saw grass out of his way as he waded back to where the stranded pup was tangled. "Be a good dog, Speed Bump. I'll get you out of this mess as soon as I can. Please don't move until I cut you free." Sam edged closer to the dog. He reached over and patted his head to assure him that he was going to help. Sam put his hands under the water to feel how the dog was stuck and unable to move. Twisted fishing line and saw grasses had tightened around the pup's back legs and body, holding him tight in place. Speed Bump began to bark and whimper.

"Shush!" Sam said gently. "Please be still and I will cut these lines without hurting you. Stop wiggling and stay still now."

Speed Bump settled down to Sam's calming voice and let him cut the fishing line and weeds away. When he was almost finished, Sam tied the laundry bag cord to the dog's collar. Then he lifted the soaking wet dog out of the water. Pete, Joey, Rick, and Garth cheered loudly to see that the dog was finally rescued. Dillon, who had just arrived at the scene to meet his friends, shouted, "What's up, guys? What happened here? Sam, what are you doing in the lake with that dog?"

Joey sat up on the canvas laundry bag, which now had gobs of dry mud caked on it, as did Joey, who looked like a muddy drowned rat. "I helped, Dillon," Joey said weakly. "I lent Sam my Swiss Army penknife. It has a knife, a pair of sharp scissors, and a file on the end of a screwdriver. It's in a red metallic case. It's neat. My Dad gave it to me on my eleventh birthday. I just knew it would come in handy one day."

Pete interrupted and explained, "While we were collecting cans, we saw a poster of a lost dog. The poster said there was a twenty-five-dollar reward. We found him trapped here in the lake and Sam and Joey went to rescue him. Joey slipped off the muddy ledge and Sam had to save his life. Thanks to Sam's quick thinking, Joey is alive. Sam worked hard using Joey's Swiss Army penknife to free the dog from his tangled mess."

"Does he have a license number on his collar?" Rick asked.

"Yes," Sam replied. "He also has a tag with his owner's name and phone number written on it." He slowly waded to the shore, carefully holding Speed Bump close to his chest. As soon as Speed Bump put his feet on solid ground, he shook so hard from his nose to the tip of his tail that water, mud and weeds went flying in all directions. The boys had to jump out of the way to avoid the muddy shower.

"How do you feel now, kid?" Rick asked his brother. "Can you ride your bike?"

"I'm okay. I think I can ride," Joey said, although he was covered in mud and looked liked a drowned rat.

"I love you, brother," Rick lectured, "and God loves you, too. You should be thankful that God didn't let you drown. He even sent a Guardian Angel to look after you. He knows you need His help, but Joey, you must think clearly and plan first before you try anything."

"Let's ride over to the phone booth," Pete suggested, "We can call Speed Bump's owner. I'm sure that he'll be glad to get his dog back safe and sound."

"Let's take a picture of him," Dillon suggested. "I see a camera on the grass. Whose is it?"

"It's mine," Joey said, "but you can use it, Dillon. If you take a picture of Speed Bump, it will look great in the F.B.I. Club's scrapbook. It'll prove that the investigation was solved."

"That's a great idea," Rick said. "Joey, are you sure it's okay if we use your camera?"

"Go ahead," Joey replied proudly, hoping this would get him into the club. Now, he could finally make a contribution to the club with his camera. "Take a close-up photo of that wet, muddy dog. Then we'll collect the reward for him."

"After you take the picture," Sam said, "I'll put Speed Bump in the basket on my bike. It's deep enough to hold him. He shouldn't jump out after all he's been through today."

The five Junior Investigators and Joey rode to the phone booth to call Mr. Cutchins, the dog's owner. Although Joey was not considered a member of the F.B.I. Club yet, he was determined to be part of the action. Rick put the money in the pay phone coin slot. Sam dialed the phone number on the dog tag. After three rings, a man answered the phone. "Are you Mr. Cutchins?" Sam inquired.

"Yes, I am," the man on the phone replied. "What can I do for you?"

"Did you lose something of value?" Sam asked.

"Yes," Mr. Cutchins replied. "I lost my dog. We were at the park couple of days ago. I took his leash off for just a few minutes and he disappeared. Do you know anything of his whereabouts?"

"Yes," Sam answered proudly. "We are the F.B.I. Club, the Famous Boy Investigators Club, and we found your dog. He was in the lake and tangled up in some weeds and fishing line. We rescued him and we have him here at the park. He's wet and muddy, but otherwise in good condition. Are you still offering the reward?"

"Yes, sir!" Mr. Cutchins replied excitedly. "I would be happy to pay the reward! I live alone and Speed Bump is my only companion. I found him when he was a puppy. His mother had her puppies in a hole in the ground, and someone ran over him and put tire marks on his back. I nursed him back to health. Now, he takes care of me by helping me exercise at the park every day."

"Do you want to come and get him?" Sam asked.

"Please stay at the phone booth and I'll be there right away," Mr. Cutchins replied.

"Okay," Sam said as he hung up the phone. "After we return the dog, we'll still have plenty of time to meet Pete's brother Tom. Remember, he will pick us up at the park's entrance and take us to the recycling center."

"We still have two empty bags. Shall we ride over to the supermarket and see if we can fill up these other two bags with cans?" Dillon asked.

"That's a good idea," Rick said. "Sam and I will stay here with Speed Bump until Mr. Cutchins arrives, and then we'll wait by the park entrance for Tom. He'll be here soon and we'll ride over to the supermarket with him, okay? I think he can put our bikes in the back of his truck with the cans."

"I want to stay here with Speed Bump," Joey protested. "I'll wait for Mr. Cutchins. I can collect the reward and bring it with me."

"Quit acting like a baby! Don't forget that Dad told you to listen to me. You're part of this project only because Dad made me take you along. If you want to be a Junior Investigator, you had better start acting like one."

"But I want an important job," Joey pleaded. "You never let me do anything important."

"One day you will have an important job, but not today," Rick replied, with his hands on his hips. "I'm President of the F.B.I. Club and I handle all the important matters. Sam is Vice President and that's why he's staying with me. Sam and I will keep the full bags of cans, here with us, while we wait with Speed Bump. You boys can't tote these heavy bags on your bikes over to the supermarket. Joey, you can go with the others and that will be your job."

"I want an important job sometime," Joey said, frowning, as he mounted his bike and rode off with Pete, Dillon and Garth. Rick, Sam, and Speed Bump waited by the phone booth. In a few minutes, Mr. Cutchins drove up to where

Rick, Sam and Speed Bump stood. Speed Bump wagged his tail and barked happily to see his owner.

"Thank you so very much," Mr. Cutchins said, almost in tears. "I never knew how much I missed this rascal until he was lost. Where exactly did you say you found him? I searched for an hour looking for him, but he was nowhere that I could see so I went home very sad." The boys told Mr. Cutchins about all the exciting events that had taken place in rescuing Speed Bump from his misadventure.

Mr. Cutchins scooped up the muddy dog and squeezed him ever so tightly. Speed Bump washed his owner's face with kisses.

"I can't thank you boys enough for rescuing my beloved Speed Bump," Mr. Cutchins said with tears in his eyes. "Here is your reward." He handed Rick an envelope that contained the twenty-five dollars. Seeing how wet Sam was, Mr. Cutchins reached for his wallet and gave Sam another twenty-five dollars for freeing Speed Bump from his tangled mess.

"But, Mr. Cutchins," Sam said, "the reward was only supposed to be twenty-five dollars."

Mr. Cutchins replied, "The first twenty five dollars was for finding Speed Bump. This second twenty-five dollars was for saving Speed Bump's life. I see you are still wet and muddy from going into the lake. You boys should get into some dry clothes as soon as possible, before you get a cold or something worse than that."

"We will, Mr. Cutchins. Thank you very much for paying us the reward," Sam said. "We will use this money to help build a tree house for our F.B.I. Club."

Rick offered Mr. Cutchins the cord from his canvas laundry bag that they were using as a temporary leash, but Mr. Cutchins had his own leash with him. He promptly attached it to Speed Bump's collar. Then he returned the laundry bag cord to Rick.

Rick, Sam, and Mr. Cutchins said their good-byes as Mr. Cutchins headed toward his car. Rick and Sam were filled with joy to see how happy Speed Bump was to be reunited with his owner. Mr. Cutchins opened the back car door. In a flash, Speed Bump jumped into the back seat. Rick and Sam were feeling confident of a job well done. They laughed as they observed the happy, muddy dog with his wet nose pressed against the window glass and his owner driving out of the park.

Soon, Tom Davis drove up to the park entrance. "Do you guys need a ride to catch up with the other boys?" Tom asked.

"Sure thing, Tom," Rick replied. "We could use a ride."

"Put your bikes in the back and hop in," Tom advised.

Then Tom got out of the truck and loaded the heavy bags of cans into the truck bed.

"I hope we get enough money for these cans to help build our tree house," Sam said.

"I hope so, too," Tom replied, "because I wouldn't want to clean out garages. It is a messy and dangerous job. It's not worth the effort for the small amount you earn."

Soon, Rick, Sam, and Tom arrived at the market where Joey, Pete, Garth, and Dillon were filling grocery bags with empty soda cans.

"Hey, guys," Tom said. "You really made a good haul. Let's get to the recycling center before they close. I think this project was a success."

"Thanks, Tom," Pete said. "I hope we got enough cash to put our share into the tree house."

Rick and Tom went to the window at the recycling center. "Excuse me, sir. What is the price of aluminum cans today?" Rick asked.

"The price today is fifty-five cents a pound," the man answered.

"Do you know how many cans it takes to make a pound?" Tom asked.

"Yes, sir, I do," the paymaster replied. "It takes 24 smashed cans to make one pound. If you happen to use a large green lawn bag, they usually hold about twenty pounds each. So the price of fifty-five cents a pound multiplied by twenty pounds would be approximately $11.00 per bag. How many bags do you have?"

"We have four large green lawn bags, two large laundry bags, and six paper grocery bags," Rick said proudly.

"Well, boys, just bring in your bags. The scale will record the weight. Then I'll pay you what's printed on the ticket. It looks like you boys have been busy," the paymaster said with a grin.

Rick looked at the ticket that printed from the scale. "We're in good shape," he said. "According to the ticket, we raised one hundred eight dollars and thirty-five cents. Wow!" All the boys jumped into the air and cheered for their accomplishment.

"Now, let's see how much money we have altogether. Fifty-dollar reward from Speed Bump, forty dollars from cleaning up at the construction sites.... When you add the recycling money, that's a total of one hundred ninety-eight dollars and thirty-five cents. I'm happy to say, we're on our way."

"Hip Hip Hurray! Three cheers for the F.B.I. club house," the boys cheered.

"Then, all we need to do is to work on building the tree house," Rick stated.

"Let's go home and call all of our friends and ask them to help us gather more aluminum cans. I'm sure that my dad would help," Dillon said.

"I'll ask at work," Tom said. "Maybe I can organize a collection of cans for you. I see them lying around all over the place in the break room."

"My dad told me about the large barrel of empty cans at the bowling alley," Rick said. "Wouldn't it be nice if he could get those cans for us? That would give us more than the $500.00 we need to build the tree house."

chapter three

THE TREE HOUSE

Rick and Joey were anxious to get home from the recycling center. Tom drove to the homes of Sam, Garth, Dillon, Rick and Joey and his brother, Pete. They were excited because their first day of gathering aluminum cans had been so successful. Each tired boy took his bike off the back of the truck as Tom congratulated them for their efforts on a job well done.

Joey ran into the kitchen yelling excitedly, "Mom, Mom, we made lots of money selling the aluminum cans!" Joey pulled a piece of paper from his jacket pocket and began to read. "The paymaster gave us $108.35 for all our cans. Sam and Rick got twenty-five dollars each for finding and rescuing a lost dog. Rick and Sam also got forty dollars for cleaning up a construction site. That makes $248.35 altogether. Rick said we need five hundred dollars to build the tree house. Do you know anyone who could help us collect more cans?"

"Settle down, son," Mother replied. "I'm so proud of you and the other boys for working so hard on your project. First, tell me what in the world happened to you! You're covered in mud, and look at your matted hair! Are those the new white cargo pants I bought you for Sunday School? Give me the details while I get you some clean clothes. I'm not sure if you will ever come clean again."

"But Mom, we were gathering cans, and we saw a poster for a lost dog. We went to investigate and found the stranded pup. Sam went into the lake to get him but he didn't have a penknife to cut away the weeds and other stuff. So, I went into the lake to give Sam my new Swiss Army penknife. Somehow I slipped off the muddy ledge and fell to the bottom of the lake. Don't worry Mom, it wasn't that deep. Sam dove under the water and pulled me to safety. It was no big deal. I don't know how all this mud got on my clothes and all over me, but Rick was there and he helped me clean up. So that's about all there is to the story," Joey told his mother innocently.

"Get to the bathroom as fast as you can and see if a shower will take the mud away. Make sure you scrub your hair. If you have a problem, call me," Mom instructed her son.

As Joey hopped off to the bathroom, he was still talking to his mother. "They paid us fifty-five cents a pound and we had 197 pounds of crushed cans," Joey said breathlessly. "Can you believe that?" As he disappeared behind the bathroom door, Joey was still shouting and continued talking over the sound of the running water. "Dad said he knew of some cans that were at the bowling alley. Do you think he might help us out?"

"I'll ask him when he gets home," Mom shouted in reply. Right now, you had better think about how you're going to get all that mud off of yourself!"

When Dad returned home from work, Rick and Joey were waiting for him on the front porch.

"What's up, boys?" Dad asked, wondering what was so important that they had to meet him before he could even get in the door. "Are you boys waiting for me?"

"Yes, Dad," Joey said excitedly. "We have great news! We got $108.35 for our aluminum cans. That was fifty-five cents a pound.

"I'm surprised and happy for the F.B.I. Club. It was worth all the work you boys put into this project. I'm so proud of you," Dad said with a sparkle in his eye.

"We are halfway to our goal," Rick interjected. "Could you ask the man at the bowling alley if we could recycle his aluminum cans for our tree house?"

"That's right, Dad," Joey interjected. "We need two hundred fifty dollars more for building materials. Could you help us?"

"I'll get on it right after supper," Dad said. He began mumbling to himself. "Fifty-five cents a pound, that's better than what I received in the past. I was lucky to get twenty-five cents a pound twenty years ago."

After supper, Dad called the bowling alley. The owner agreed to give the boys one barrel of cans because he was so proud of their willingness to work for a project. He said he normally held the empty cans until the price went up so he could make a profit.

The next afternoon Sam, Pete and Dillon rode their bikes to Rick's back yard.

"Hey, guys," Rick said to the boys, "my dad spoke to the owner at the bowling alley. He said we could have all the cans that would fit into one barrel. Let's go over there now and collect them. That should bring in a lot of cash for the tree house."

"Sure thing," Pete said. "Let's go. I have plenty of lawn bags in the basket on my bike. Let me call my brother Tom and ask him to drive us to the recycling center. We'll need his help to empty the barrel of aluminum cans. Can I use your phone, Rick?"

Pete borrowed Rick's phone and dialed. "Hello, Tom, can you meet us boys of the F.B.I. Club over at the bowling alley?" Pete asked. "The owner said we could have all the cans in one barrel. We're ready to go over there. Can you drive us to the recycling center?"

Pete hung up the phone and announced, "Tom said he would meet us in about thirty minutes so if we hurry, we can have all the cans bagged and be on our way to the recycling center. That should raise the amount of cash we need. Boy, am I excited! I didn't think we could do it, but now I think we'll have enough money to build our tree house."

When the boys finished bagging the cans, Tom came into the bowling alley to inspect the haul. "Good job, boys. Help me put these bags in the back of the truck. I think there will be enough room left to put your bikes."

At the recycling center, the paymaster, Mr. Wind, saw the boys and waved to them. "Put your cans in the hopper and let's see how much they weigh."

"Is the price still fifty-five cents a pound?" Rick asked.

"Sure is," said Mr. Wind. "Your total for today is forty-and-a-half pounds, for two hundred and twenty-five dollars. You boys will have enough to build that tree house pretty soon."

Back at Rick's house, the boys talked excitedly about how close they were to being able to start building the tree house. "I bet we can build it in one day if we all work together," Pete said.

"No," Rick replied, "but we can have it built in about two days. I talked with Uncle Charlie yesterday about building the tree house. He said that if we all work together, we could finish it in about two days. He also said that he would give us some help, too, if we need it."

"Uncle Charlie is a construction engineer and knows how to build houses. He is the best person to help us build the tree house," Pete told Rick, as he handed over a small donation of fifteen dollars from his Uncle Charlie to help purchase the materials.

"We haven't heard from Justin yet," Rick said. "I'll call him, and then we can get started with this adventure!" Rick headed into the house and told the guys he'd be back in a minute. When the phone call was completed, Rick went outside to tell the others. "Justin said he would be here shortly with the money he's earned. He said his parents gave him twenty-five dollars for cleaning and washing both of their cars. Dillon wasn't home, but I told his mother that we were going to the Mayfield Lumber Yard. He'll be home soon and try to meet us there."

"Are you all ready to go to the Mayfield Lumber Yard to order the materials for the tree house?" Dad asked. "Do you have enough money to pay for everything?"

"Yes, we are ready to go and we have enough money." Rick said, "We're just waiting for Garth to get here, then we'll be on our way. I think we have enough money to pay for everything. I added up all the cash. It comes to five hundred and five dollars and thirty-five cents. When Sam checked the prices at the lumber yard, the salesman assured him that it would not go over five hundred dollars."

The phone rang while the boys were outside talking to Mr. Spencer. "Rick, this call is for you," Mom said. "Come inside." She handed Rick the phone. "I think it's Justin Stewart."

"Hi, Justin," Rick said into the phone. "What's up? Where are you? We're all ready to go to the Mayfield Lumber Yard.

We're going to order the supplies and materials for the tree house. Are you going to go with us?" Rick paused, waiting for an answer. "That's great, we'll see you there," Rick said as he finished his phone call.

"Is he going to meet us?" Pete called as he rode his bike around in circles in the driveway.

"Yes," Rick replied. "He said he has to wait for the babysitter to take care of his little sister. He will try to meet us at the lumberyard. Let's get ready to take off. Aw, here comes Joey! I wish there were a way that I could leave him at home. He's always getting into trouble."

"Joey isn't that bad," Pete said. "I always get stuck sitting with my twin cousins. They are three years old and they are a lot more trouble than Joey."

"It's just that Joey always gets into some kind of trouble. He just won't listen. Worst of all, my parents make me take him with me. Bummer!" Rick told the group.

Garth rode into the driveway. "I'm not too late, am I?" Garth said as he got off his bike and checked the chain around the wheel.

"Not now," Rick said. With the cash in hand, Rick, Joey, Pete, Sam, and Garth rode their bikes across town to the Mayfield Lumber Yard to purchase the supplies and materials for the tree house. Justin and Dillon were waiting in the parking lot for their friends.

"Did you remember that we need to buy a hank of rope? We can use it with the block and tackle to pull the boards up into the branches of the oak tree," Justin said.

"Yes, I sure did," Rick replied, "It's on the list of materials and supplies."

When they went into the Mayfield Lumber Yard, a salesman greeted them. Rick gave him the list of materials and asked, "Could you deliver the materials Saturday morning? We're going to build a tree house in my back yard."

"Are you sure of the measurements, especially the floor boards?" the salesman questioned. "You know that you must be accurate. Did you have the branches checked to make sure they're strong enough to hold the tree house?"

"No," Rick replied. "The branches looked strong enough."

"Do you know of anyone in the construction business or a tree surgeon who could examine the tree before you spend all of this money?" the salesman inquired.

Pete spoke up. "My Uncle Charlie has a construction business. He is going to help us build the tree house."

"Please consult with him. Ask him if the branches are strong enough to hold the weight of the lumber and you boys, too," the salesman suggested.

"That makes sense," Rick replied. "Pete, will you call your Uncle Charlie and ask him if he could check out the tree today?"

"Okay, I'll call him from here," Pete said as he looked around for a pay phone.

The salesman led the boys to the store phone. Pete dialed the number, and Uncle Charlie answered on the third ring.

"Uncle Charlie, this is Pete. We boys of the F.B.I. Club have a problem. We have earned the money to pay for the materials for the tree house, but the salesman said that we should have the branches tested to be sure that they will hold the tree house and all of us, too. We also have to check the measurements because when they deliver the material to us, we can't return anything that is cut wrong because of incorrect measurements. Could you check it out today?"

Pete listened for a moment and then said, "That's great! Uncle Charlie, would you please call the Mayfield Lumber Yard and speak to the lumber salesman, Mr. Tolson? Then he'll fill our order and have it delivered tomorrow so we can get started building the tree house. Will you be there, too?"

Pete listened again, thanked his uncle and hung up. He told his friends, "Uncle Charlie said he'll check it out for us this afternoon. He has a roofing job two doors down from Rick's, so he'll be in the neighborhood."

By the time the boys returned to Rick's house, Uncle Charlie had arrived and taken the long extension ladder off the truck. Uncle Charlie looked up into the tree. "Did you boys know that the best place to put this tree house is almost as high as your second-story window?" He put the ladder against the tree and pushed it up until it rested on the spot where the branches separated to form a base. He climbed up, looked around, and called down to Pete and the boys, "These branches are healthy, and as large as they are, two feet in diameter, this tree will easily hold a house. Your tree house will be secure. Now let's check the measurements to be sure they're accurate."

"I'm the tallest and we're all here to help you if you need anything," Sam volunteered.

"Sure thing, son," Uncle Charlie answered. "Sam, will you bring up the six-foot level from the bed of the truck? Be careful that you don't drop it or fall off the ladder."

"Not to worry, Uncle Charlie," Sam replied. "I think I'm tall enough to handle this job." When he neared the top of the ladder, he was happy to see that the main branches were very thick and strong. He handed the level to Uncle Charlie, who crawled out over the branches to the opposite side of the tree.

"Hold the level steady so I can make sure the floor will fit evenly," Uncle Charlie instructed. "The lumber yard will cut the boards so we must be accurate with our measurements." Uncle Charlie reached across and handed Sam the end of the tape measure. "Will you hold the tape measure for me, too?"

"Sure thing," Sam replied. "I didn't realize how much work was involved in preparing to build a tree house," Sam said as he held the tape measure steady.

"Well, I'll be a monkey's uncle!" Uncle Charlie remarked. "The floor will be exactly eight feet square. We won't have to make any other changes. I'll call Mr. Tolson at the lumber yard and give him the final measurements. They should be able to deliver the materials tomorrow."

"Thanks a lot, Uncle Charlie, you're the best," Sam said as he went down the ladder. He paused when he was halfway down to get a good hold on the level, and carried it to the ground.

"Thanks, Uncle Charlie," Rick, Joey, Pete, and Dillon called out in unison. "Our dream is about to come true."

Before Uncle Charlie left he cautioned, "Don't be climbing up this tree unless there is someone else with you. If you fall, you will surely break some bones. Do you all understand? I'm going to leave my ladder here because you'll need it tomorrow."

"Yes sir," Rick replied. "We'll be careful. We'll always use the buddy system."

The boys went into the house to get a drink of cold milk and a peanut butter sandwich.

"Where's Joey?" Mom asked.

"I don't know," Pete replied. "I thought he was behind us."

"I hope he didn't climb that tree!" Rick said, fearful of what Joey could do. "Uncle Charlie told us not to go up alone, but you know Joey doesn't listen very well."

"I'd better go out and check," Sam volunteered. As soon as Sam walked onto the porch, he knew that Joey was in trouble again. He noticed first that Uncle Charlie's ladder had fallen to the ground.

"Help! Help!" Joey squealed, hanging with his arms and legs wrapped around the tree branch. "Help! Help! Help! Sam, get me down from here!!"

"Hold on, buddy, I'm going to get help!" Sam yelled as he ran into the house. "Come quickly before Joey falls out of the tree. Hurry, everybody!" he said breathlessly. "Joey's hanging upside down from the skinny branches. He's gonna fall down and break his neck!"

Mom ran out the kitchen door, wiping her hands on her apron. "Hold on Joey! We'll get you down. Weren't you told to stay out of the tree?"

"Rick, go call the fire department and ask them to come fast before this rascal falls out of the tree," Mom said, as she watched her precious child hanging with his arms and legs wrapped around the limb of the oak tree.

"Don't worry, Mom," Joey assured her. "My arms and legs are strong. I don't know how Uncle Charlie's ladder fell, but it just fell away from the tree and here I am. I don't know how to get down."

Sam and Rick picked up the fallen ladder and put it against the tree. Sam was just beginning to climb the ladder when they heard the fire engine sirens.

"We better not try to help Joey," Rick said "Help is on the way and we don't know how to get him down either."

The fire truck pulled up into the driveway. Pete and Dillon rushed to tell the firemen that Joey was in the back yard stuck in a tree. The Fire Chief, Captain Donnie Manning, took one look at Joey in his very unsafe position. "Oh, my, the bucket truck is off at another call. We will have to use the Steeple Method to get this child down out of the tree."

"What's the Steeple Method?" Dillon asked, scared of what might happen to his friend.

"The Steeple Method," Chief Manning continued, "is when a ladder is held straight up and secured with two ropes that hold the ladder secure against the branch." Captain Manning instructed his two firemen to move the extension ladder to where Joey was hanging. Captain Manning climbed the ladder. He told Joey to let his legs loose and put them on the rungs of the ladder.

"I'm scarified," Joey cried. "I don't want to fall like Humpty Dumpty."

"Don't panic, son," Captain Manning assured Joey. "I'm here to help you."

"I can't do it," Joey pleaded. "If I let my legs go, then my arms will go too and I'll splatter all over the ground."

Captain Manning put his arms around Joey and assured him that he would not let him fall to the ground. With encouragement from Captain Manning, Joey released his legs from around the branch. Captain Manning held him securely, and they both went down the ladder to the ground below.

Joey's knees were shaking so badly that Captain Manning had to hold him tightly so he could stand on his wobbly legs.

Captain Manning said sternly, "Son that was not a very smart thing to do. You must always have a buddy with you. You not only pulled the firemen away from their duties, but you also could be lying injured on the ground and no one would find you until it was too late."

Mom said, her voice shaking, "We will just ground you until your father comes back from the store. Now, go to your room!"

As dad was returning from the store, he was shocked to see the fire truck leaving the back yard. "What happened here?" Dad inquired nervously.

Rick told dad about the incident. "See, Dad, he's always getting into trouble. He could have been killed. I don't know what to do."

Dad went up to Joey's bedroom for a serious talk. "Joey," Dad said firmly, "don't you want to be part of this project? I am so disappointed in you, because we had an agreement that you would stay out of trouble and now look at you."

"I'm sorry, Dad," Joey apologized. "I'll think before I do anything again. I really want to be a part of the construction project. Can I still help with the tree house?"

"You must stay on the ground until further notice. You must prove to me that you are responsible enough to help with the construction," Dad replied. "No more funny business."

*****

Bright and early Saturday morning, the lumber yard's truck pulled into the driveway. The men unloaded all of the supplies. Justin, Dillon, and Pete were surprised to see so much wood, nails, shingles, and rope being piled up next to the oak tree.

Detective Spencer came out the kitchen door. "Well boys, I have some bad news for you. I just talked to Uncle Charlie, and he told me that it looks like you will have to build the tree house by yourselves. Uncle Charlie has to finish the roof up the street. He won't have time to help. Sam's dad, Mr. Davis, was called out on a job, but I'll be here in case you need me."

"Not to worry, dad," Rick replied. "We can do it ourselves. Remember we have detailed plans, and Garth is experienced. I'm glad that you'll be here in case we need you. Thanks Dad. You're the best!"

"Mom suggested that I get the grill going so we can have a cookout for lunch. How does that suit you?" Dad asked, rubbing his stomach and clanging the grilling tools together.

"Sounds good to me," Rick replied. "The smell of the hamburgers and hot dogs cooking will make us work faster."

"Let's hold a quick meeting," Rick said to his friends. "We need to put someone in charge who knows what to do. I suggest that we put Garth in charge, since he has already built a tree house. Sam, who is tall and steady on his feet, can be his chief assistant. I can read the plans. Dillon and Justin can handle the lumber together. Pete can be my assistant. Joey can be in charge of bringing lemonade to us. He is good in the kitchen. Do I hear a vote in favor of my suggestions or do we need some discussion? Give me a yea or nay vote."

The boys all gave the yea, and the work got under way.

Dad volunteered to hold the ladder for security. He didn't want to have the firemen paying a return visit.

Garth climbed the ladder to get to the base. He had a rope with the pulley tied around his waist. He then pulled himself up to the next higher branch. He attached the pulley to the highest, strongest branch so that the rope would fall straight to the ground.

"Be careful, Garth," Sam said as he watched his pal climb up higher in the oak tree.

Garth threaded the rope through the pulley. He put the two ends of the rope together as they fell to the ground. "Hey, Pete, tie each end of this rope to a white five-gallon bucket with a double half-hitch knot, around the handle of the bucket."

"Yes, sir," Pete said as he secured the rope. He remembered how to tie a double half-hitch knot. He had earned a merit badge for tying knots when he was a Cub Scout.

Rick read the plans. They called for eight 2x8 boards. Dillon helped Pete tie the first board to the rope with a bungee cord and put the other end of the board in the bucket for safety. Justin stood on the ladder to steer the bucket and the board up into the tree. Pete pulled the rope and watched the board disappear into the green leaves.

"Thanks, I got the board!" Sam said. "Garth is on his way down after hanging the block and tackle. Next we'll nail this board to the base of the tree branches."

"Let me know when you need the next board," Justin hollered up. "We're ready when you are."

When the hammering stopped, Garth called down, "Send up the next board and keep them coming. We now have plenty room to store the boards until we nail them to the tree branches."

Within the hour, the floor was built. "Send up the wood sealer," Garth said. "We can paint the floor next. While it is drying, we can come down and help you guys put the sides together."

"Great!" Rick said. "Mom made some lemonade and her famous chocolate brownies. We can take a snack break now.

Justin, Dillon, and Pete ran into the house to get cleaned up so they could have refreshments while Rick studied the plans.

Joey got a tray and put several tall glasses of lemonade on it. He then piled on a mountain of chocolate brownies.

"Mom," Joey whined, "can't I go out and help the boys?"

"No, Joey," Mom said. "Maybe you will learn to act more responsible and listen to your elders. All you can do is deliver the snacks and then come right back to the house."

Joey grumbled as he ran out the back door. He went so fast that brownies were flying in all directions. The lemonade was splashing on the tray and on Joey's clean shirt.

"Look out, here comes a tornado. Joey's at it again!" Rick yelled. "It looks like he'll be wearing more lemonade than we'll be drinking."

A few minutes later, Joey gathered up the empty glasses and the empty brownie plate and sat on the back porch pondering on how he could convince his mother that he was a changed boy.

After the snack, the boys went back to their construction project.

"I understand what the plans mean," Rick murmured to himself. "I'll measure for the windows. Uncle Charlie left his sawhorses, safety goggles, and a bench saw. Dad is here to supervise cutting the lumber."

"Dad, we're ready to cut the windows and the door. Will you come over and help us?" Rick asked.

"Yes, son," Dad replied. "I'll be glad to help. Have you drawn the outlines?"

"When Sam and Garth came out after lunch, they checked my measurements to be sure I was correct. I used the T-square to be sure I made the window square," Rick told his Dad.

Rick checked the measurements again. The 4x8-foot sheet of painted plywood was on top of the sawhorses. The openings for the windows were drawn in black marker. Dad checked the boys for safety and instructed Justin how to saw the openings while Pete and Dillon held the wall panel steady.

Later in the day, Uncle Charlie pulled into the driveway. "Howdy boys, I just stopped by to check on your progress and see if there is anything I can do to help you."

"Well," Rick said, "we finished the floor. Sam and Garth painted the floor with a water sealer. Garth checked the floor with the level in all four directions to make sure that it was okay. In the meantime, Justin, Pete, and I painted the inside and outside of the four walls with water sealer so the wood wouldn't rot. The plywood sides are leaning against the fence now to dry. Dillon painted all the window frames inside and out with the white house paint that you left at Pete's house last year.

"The work looks very good, boys," Uncle Charlie said. "It's getting late, so you need to stop for today and let the paint dry. Tomorrow will be soon enough to put it all together. Do you have the shingles nailed to the roof sections?"

"Yes, sir," Justin said as he walked over to meet Uncle Charlie. "I nailed the roof shingles just as you told me. I started at the bottom and followed the lines until I got to the top. I even have the roof cap ready. How soon do we put the sides on?"

"No need to hurry the job, Justin," Uncle Charlie said. "We have to wait until the paint dries, so I suggest that you boys relax for now. Tomorrow is another day."

"Can we have a sleepover?" Joey asked from the porch.

"Even if we decide to have a sleepover, you can't be part of it because you're grounded," Rick said. "And no funny business either."

"Where would you sleep?" Joey asked, snickering. "The floor in the tree house is wet. See, you can't have a sleepover anyhow."

"Let's get cleaned up and ask our parents if we can have a sleepover," Dillon said. "I don't think it's going to rain tonight, so maybe we can sleep under the stars. What do you guys think?"

Rick began thinking about the sleepover and how to get away from his troublemaking brother Joey.

"I've got an idea," Garth said, rubbing his brow as he gathered his thoughts. "Our scout troop has a tent that is ten foot square. I'll call Mr. Byrum, my scoutmaster, and ask him if we could borrow the tent. I think he would let us use it for just one night, and we'd be ready to go to work in the morning," Garth said.

"Good idea! Sleeping in the tent will keep the bugs off of us, too," Pete added. "My brother Tom has a truck. I can ask him to go with you and get the tent. Can you call your scoutmaster now?"

"Rick, can I use your phone?" Garth asked.

"Sure," Rick replied. "The cordless phone is in the kitchen. Let us know what he says, okay?"

"No problem," Garth replied as he dialed his scoutmaster's number. In a few rings, Mr. Byrum answered.

"Thanks, Mr. Byrum, for lending us the tent," Garth replied into the phone. "I think I have a ride over to your house to pick up the tent. We promise to return it tomorrow afternoon. See you soon."

"Okay Pete, call your brother and ask if he can drive me to Mr. Byrum's house," Garth said proudly.

"Sure thing," Pete said as he dialed his home, hoping that Tom would be home from work by now. "Hello, Tom," Pete said. "We want to have a sleepover at Rick's house tonight, but we need to get a tent from Mr. Byrum, the scoutmaster on Sycamore Street. Can you ride Garth over to Mr. Byrum's house, pick up the tent and bring it back to Rick's house? Pete paused, listening to Tom's response. "Thanks Tom. Garth and I will be waiting in front of Rick's house. See you in a few minutes."

Pete and Garth got washed up and ready to go get the tent. Joey came out of the house and asked if he could go along for the ride. "I won't get into any trouble," Joey promised. "I'm just so bored sitting here at home alone."

"Go ask your mother," Justin said. "I won't be responsible for you."

In a few minutes, Joey came out the door with his head hanging low. "My mom said I can't go with you, but maybe I can sleep with you guys in the tent."

"We'll see about that when the time comes, Joey," Pete said. "I wouldn't hold my breath on that one. I think your brother is still upset with you."

In a short time, Garth, Pete, and Tom returned to Rick's house. They all worked together, like a well-oiled machine. They quickly assembled the tent in the backyard. When it was finished, Tom asked, "Do you all have your sleeping bags here?"

"I don't have mine yet," Garth said. "I need to go home and get it, Tom. Would you mind dropping me off at my house? My dad can bring me back. Thanks again for your help, Tom. You are a true friend to all of us Junior Investigators."

"Glad to do it," Tom replied. "I remember when I had sleepovers. Boy, those were great times."

"Thanks again for your help, Tom," Garth replied gratefully. "You are a true friend to all of us in the F.B.I. Club."

In a little while, Garth came back with a bucket of Kentucky Fried Chicken and a bag of side orders. He also had his sleeping bag around his shoulder and over his back. He entered the kitchen and put the KFC with the side orders on the counter. "My mom thought because we worked so hard we might just be hungry. This is my mom's treat for the F.B.I. club. Does anyone have the sodas?"

"I do," Joey said quickly. "Uncle Gus gave me a case of sodas in a cooler. I can bring them now. They're really cold, too."

"Even though you have the sodas, you can't be part of the F.B.I. Club," Rick said.

"Oh, Rick," Mom said, "that's not fair. He has made his contribution the same as everyone else. Please reconsider and let him eat in the tent with the rest of the boys."

After much thinking, Rick reconsidered and said, "I guess it'll be okay, but that's all. He can't sleep in the tent with us. That's for members only."

Everyone went to the tent. Justin passed out the napkins. Joey arrived with the sodas, his face beaming with pride. Pete poured the sodas in large plastic glasses while Sam put lids on them. Joey came out of the house with six wet washcloths and a roll of paper towels for the cleanup. Dillon got a trash bag to keep the tent clean.

After a hearty supper, the boys stretched out their sleeping bags and sat around thinking about how they would put the sides and roof on the tree house. Soon darkness fell and the boys yawned one by one.

"Okay, Joey," Rick said. "The party is over, so you'd better go in the house and sleep in your own room."

"Please let me stay, Rick," Joey pleaded. "I'll be good and not cause any trouble."

"Do as I told you," Rick said "You may be eleven years old, but you act like a two-year-old. First, you need to grow up." Rick started to get up and escort Joey out of the tent.

"You'll be sorry for this," Joey said as he left the tent and stomped back into the house.

"What do you think Joey has on his mind this time?" Sam asked.

"It's probably something devious," Dillon answered. "He is a piece of work. I guess he just wants a lot of attention. Doesn't he have friends of his own?"

"Yes, he does, but they're just as bad as he is," Rick said, shaking his head. "I don't want him in the F.B.I. Club until he can act his age and be responsible for his actions."

"I'm tired," Justin said as he yawned. "We'd better get a good night's sleep. We have a lot of work to do tomorrow." In no time at all, all five of the boys were sound asleep and dreaming of the next day's work and hopefully the completion of the tree house.

Joey looked out of his bedroom window. He waited until he didn't see any movement. Then he tiptoed down the stairs and gently opened the back door. "I'll fix those boys!" he thought. "If they won't let me sleep in the tent, then why should I let them sleep in there either?" Joey crept over to the water hose that was neatly wrapped up next to one of the spigots. Then he turned on the water full blast. He twisted the spray nozzle until it began to give a wide spray, and he aimed the streaming water spray at the tent. All of a sudden the five boys felt the water entering the tent through the nylon mesh windows. They were wet from their heads to their toes. Their sleeping bags became a soggy mess, too.

"Hey! What's going on?" Dillon screamed. "Is that you, Joey?"

Rick jumped up and tripped over his wet sleeping bag. He ran out of the tent and saw his brother still holding the gushing garden hose. "Joey, I'm going to knock your block off if you don't get out of my sight right NOW!"

Sam, Pete, and Garth stood up and hollered at Joey, "Get out of here, kid, before we get hold of you." Justin said angrily, "Don't you know that I'm a wrestling champion? You don't want to mess with me."

In a few minutes, the lights in the house came on and Dad came out on the back porch.

"What is all the ruckus about? Will somebody tell me what's going on?" Dad demanded.

"It's just Joey being Joey," Rick said angrily. "He ruined our sleepover. I sent him to his room when we were ready to go to sleep and this is what he did. I had told him already that the sleepover was for members only and he couldn't sleep with us. At least I let him eat with us in the tent, and this is how he treated us. He turned the water hose on full blast and got all of us soaking wet and our sleeping bags, too. Not only that, Dad, but we also promised Mr. Byrum, Garth's scoutmaster, that we would return the tent tomorrow. Now I don't know how we can do that—it's soaking wet! I told you, Dad, you never know what he's going to do next. Can you put him in jail until we get this tree house built?"

"I don't think jail is the answer, but I will deal with Joey. First of all, you boys need to come in the house and get dried off. Then I'll get some rags and a mop to soak up the water in the tent. Next I'll get a heater to dry off the inside of the tent. If it isn't dry by noon tomorrow, I will call Mr. Byrum and explain the situation. I'm sure he'll understand."

Mom came out of the kitchen door carrying an armload of bath towels. "Here boys, get dried off. I put a quilt and a blanket on Rick's bedroom floor for each of you. You'd better get some rest now, because tomorrow will be a big day for all of you. Leave your wet clothes by the dryer and I'll dry them for you.

Joey tiptoed down the stairs and went to his dad. "Dad, I'm sorry, "Joey said sheepishly. "I only turned the water hose on the boys because they wouldn't let me sleep in the tent with them. It's all their fault because they wouldn't let me join in. If they had let me sleep with them, I wouldn't have sprayed them."

"Well, young man," Dad said in a firm voice. "First of all, that was not a good excuse for what you did. I don't know what to do with you, son. You make promises and then you don't keep them. So you will have to help your mother and stay on the ground until the tree house is completed."

"I want to be a junior investigator and Rick won't let me join," Joey complained.

"You knew the rules. You have to be eleven-and-a-half years old. You must also know that friendship is earned," Dad said. "You can't make someone like you. But you can act grown up enough to gain their trust. Then they might want you in their club. If you keep causing trouble, no one will want you in their group. Remember, you can catch more bees with sugar than you can with vinegar. It's the same with friendship. Do you understand, son?"

"Yes, I think so Dad," Joey said sadly. "I'll be good and use the sugar method on these boys. Dad, it is so very hard being eleven!"

"Son, go to your room now. I want you to sit down and pray. Ask God to help you be a good boy. God will answer your prayers. Do you think you can do that? Remember that you learned how to pray in Sunday School. Now all you have to do is put it to work."

"I think I can do that," Joey said. "Geez, Dad, I never knew it would be this hard growing up." When Joey returned to his bedroom, he bowed his head, folded his hands and asked God to help him grow up and not mess up again.

Everyone dried off, settled down, and went back to sleep on the soft quilts on Rick's bedroom floor. .

****

When the sun came up, a warm breeze came in through the open window. They yawned, stretched and got up to face a new day of adventure. The tree house would finally become a reality.

After dressing in dry clothes, the boys came into the kitchen. Joey was setting the table. "Hi, guys, are you ready for breakfast? Mom, Dad, and I had a long talk last night. I'm sorry for spraying you guys with water. Today, I'm going to show all of you that I'm mature and responsible enough to be a Junior Investigator. I told Mom and Dad that I would serve you breakfast this morning. I have raisin toast, Cheerios, O.J. and anything else you want as long as I don't have to cook it."

"Thanks," Rick said, acknowledging Joey. He was not really sure whether Joey was serious about his offer.

Garth, Dillon, Sam, and Pete shouted in unison. "I want Cheerios!" They all looked at each other with surprise and began to laugh.

After breakfast, the boys went right to work. Rick read the plans. Sam and Garth climbed the ladder and checked the floor that was now dry. Garth called down to the guys below. "Send up the first wall panel, we're ready."

Now that the door and the windows had been cut out, the windowsills could be completed. The windowsills were cut out of 2x4s so they could be nailed in place, and then the sidewalls were ready to be installed.

As lunchtime approached, Dad came out to get the grill started. He looked at how well all the boys were working with each other. He paused, smiled, and told the boys that he was so very pleased with the job. "I would be glad to continue to offer any advice, except please don't ask me to climb the ladder. It's just not my cup of tea."

The sun was bright. The weather was so warm that the paint dried quickly on the plywood. Justin painted the outside of the panels, as well as the windowsills, with white house paint. Pete and Dillon tied the rope securely around the first panel.

Pete called up to Garth and Sam, "Justin and I are sending up the boxes of nails. The boxes are in the white bucket. You can pull on the rope now to bring the nails up to your workspace."

After receiving the nails, the wall panels were lifted next. Garth sat on one branch and Sam sat on another waiting for the wall panel to be hoisted up to them. Justin grabbed hold of the rope and started pulling, pulling, and pulling the rope. The large, wide panels rose up, up, and up in the air.

Justin called out, "Joey, I need your help. This panel is heavier than I thought!" Joey was filled with excitement just to be asked to participate in the project. His face beamed with joy as he grabbed the rope with Justin. The two boys were pulling on the rope hand-over-hand. Mr. Spencer was supervising all of the activity while he was cooking on the grill. "You boys be careful," Mr. Spencer cautioned. "Don't let that panel knock you off the platform. Rick, why don't you help Joey and Justin?"

The three boys pulled and pulled on the rope until the panel was hoisted above the platform.

"That's high enough," Garth called to the ground. "Sam and I will take it from here." They untied the panel from the rope. Carefully, the two boys walked the panel to the edge of the platform. While standing on the platform, they moved the panel until it was flush with the edge. Garth steadied the panel while Sam nailed it in place. They did the same to panels two, three, and finally panel four where the front door would fit. They used the T-square to be sure all the corners were square. Then they hauled up the four pieces of the roof with the shingles nailed in place, and nailed them to the sides. This gave them a two-foot overhang so that rain wouldn't fall in the windows. When the roof was completed, Mr. Spencer moved the extension ladder, so the boys could get to the outside. Finally, the boys could put the ridge cap over the peak of the roof.

"That just about does it," Garth said. "Gee, teamwork is wonderful. We built this tree house in two days. All we need now is a few finishing touches."

"Yeah, like windows, a door, and a clean place to lie down," Dillon said, looking at the inside of the club house after he had climbed the ladder.

"Not to worry," Justin said. "I carefully painted the window frames yesterday. I didn't even get any paint on the window glass."

"We can put them on after lunch," Garth said. "My stomach tells me that I'm hungry! What's for lunch?"

Joey hurried to the kitchen and brought out the paper plates, napkins, and plastic forks. "Here guys," he said as he handed utensils to everyone. "It smells like the hot dogs and hamburgers are done. Mom said the buns and the ketchup are out there on the picnic table."

The boys whispered to each other. "I think Joey really has turned over a new leaf," Dillon remarked. "He is trying hard to be good. I know prayer really works, but I never thought it worked that fast!"

"I want to believe it," Rick said, looking at Joey over Garth's shoulder. "I think I can almost see a halo around his head."

My mom believes in Guardian Angels," Pete said. "She says that everyone has a Guardian Angel looking after them. I'll bet Joey's Guardian Angel must be very tired by now."

While enjoying their lunch, Sam said, "What we really need is a fire escape ladder. My dad works for the fire department and he can get a discount. I'm sure he will let us use ours from home until he can replace it with a new one. Do you guys want to come over to my house after we're done eating to see our fire escape ladder?"

Just then, Mom came outside with some more cold drinks. "How's everything going?" she asked.

They all smiled and shouted, "Okay!"

"Can I go over to Sam's, too?" Joey asked his mom.

"This is really your brother's project," Mom replied. "Let me ask him if you can go with them."

"Rick," Mom asked, "do you mind if Joey goes to Sam's with you? He is trying to be good and maybe now he has learned his lesson. What do you think? Remember you were eleven once yourself."

"Okay, Mom," Rick said with a sigh, "but this is his last chance. You had better remind him to behave."

"Thanks, Rick," Mom answered with a smile. "You sure are growing up to be a forgiving and responsible young man."

Rick, Garth, Dillon, Pete, and Joey went over to Sam's house to try out the fire escape ladder. The boys ran up the stairs to Sam's room. Sam opened the window and then demonstrated to the boys how the ladder works. First, the metal ladder hooks were fitted over the windowsill. Then,

Sam let the ladder fall to the ground. The chain sides with the metal rungs clanged as it fell to the ground.

Sam was the first one to go down the ladder. Pete was the second junior investigator to climb down. Rick was told how to put his hands and feet on the metal rungs, and then he went down the ladder. Dillon was next. "I've swung on ropes before. I used to swing out over the Tar River." He scampered down the ladder quickly.

"You're next, Joey," Sam instructed. "It will be a piece of cake as long as you don't look down."

"I don't want to get hurt when I hit the ground. I don't want to end up like Humpty Dumpty either!" Joey said, as he looked out of the window to the ground far below.

"Just hold onto the windowsill as you back out of the window," Sam said. "The rungs of the ladder are secure."

"I'm scarified!" Joey said with a trembling voice.

"You weren't scarified when you climbed the oak tree and we had to call the fire department to get you down. So don't look down now!" Sam said, as he assisted Joey to put his feet on the first rung of the ladder. "You're doing very well. Just keep your mind on what you're doing."

Joey continued down, trembling on every rung of the ladder until he reached the ground. "Whew, I don't know if that was really a piece of cake or not." Joey sighed and laughed at being so frightened.

Justin and Garth came down the ladder swiftly and remarked to Rick, Joey, and Dillon, "Now all you have to do is climb back up the ladder. It's just as easy going up as it is coming down."

"Do I have to climb up, too?" Joey asked. "I really don't want to."

"You do if you want to become a Junior Investigator and a member of the F.B.I. Club," Rick said with authority. "You also have to be eleven-and-a-half years old."

"Well," Joey answered, "I want to be a Junior Investigator, so I guess I will have to try to get back to the top."

"Whew," Joey said, as he pulled himself up rung-by-rung. The ladder swayed each time he put his foot on the next rung. He carefully moved upwards until he got to the windowsill. He crawled inside the window and collapsed on the bed to catch his breath. Then he rubbed his sore muscles from the struggle up the ladder. "After I got started, it was a piece of cake. I can do it!" But Joey still had butterflies fluttering around in his stomach. He was too proud to tell anyone his secret. He never wanted the others to know how fearful he really was.

Pete climbed the ladder without getting out of breath. "That was easy," he said with a laugh. "Do you guys want to do it again?"

"No, thank you," Rick said. "But I think it will be a great way to get up and down from the tree house."

As soon as Dillon climbed up, the boys left for home. "See you later, guys." Sam said.

When Sam's dad returned from work, he asked him if the boys of the F.B.I. Club could use the fire escape ladder for the tree house.

"That's a good idea, son," Mr. Davis remarked. "I would have suggested it when I examined the finished tree house. I am so pleased that you thought of an exit plan."

"We built the tree house in only two days. Rick read the blueprints and followed them exactly. We didn't have any problems. Mr. Spencer was always around holding the ladder. But we did a good job by ourselves. The only thing missing was the fire escape ladder. Now we can install it and the project will be completed. We will still leave Uncle Charlie's ladder for us to go up and down into the tree house."

"I'll go with you and inspect the tree house for safety and workmanship," Mr. Davis said. "I'll give you guys a certificate of occupancy if it meets all the standards for tree houses."

"Thanks, Dad," Sam said. "I'm sure that the tree house will meet all of the requirements. I think that teamwork made it a success. We're all pleased with the job and I think you will be too."

Sam and his dad went to the tree house. Mr. Davis climbed the ladder and entered through the open doorway. "You boys did a very good job. Are you sure no one else helped?" he said, admiring the workmanship. "It looks like a professional built it."

"That's right, Dad," Sam related. "We did it all by ourselves. Garth Waters was in charge because he had already built one in his own back yard. I was his assistant."

Mr. Davis came down from the tree house. All the boys gathered around him. "I can't find even one violation. I deem this tree house safe." All the boys were jumping and cheering.

Soon Uncle Gus, Uncle Charlie, and Dad came out to see the finished tree house.

"Dad," Joey said. "I think that we should say a prayer over the tree house. We need God and his Angels to look after it and protect us so we won't get hurt or anything bad like that."

Mr. Davis, Uncle Charlie, and Mr. Spencer removed their caps and folded their hands. Rick, Joey, Garth, Justin, Dillon, Sam, and Pete stood silently with their heads bowed. Mr. Spencer said a "Prayer of Blessing" for their club house. When he was finished, everyone said "Amen."

"I feel better now," Joey said. "Thanks for praying and blessing our tree house."

Uncle Charlie said, "There's enough wood left over to build a picnic table and a couple of benches. Since I already built a set for my back yard, I can build a table and benches for the tree house."

Everyone admired the tree house and how neatly they had cleaned up the area and stacked the remaining materials. They cheered because the job was completed.

"Okay, okay, boys, quiet down," Mr. Davis said in a calming voice. "My son Sam asked me for our fire escape ladder to use for an emergency exit from the tree house. I see no problem with that. Just remember, it is only for emergencies. Sam, will you get the ladder from the truck and we can finish this project."

Sam headed towards the car. "Hey Sam," Justin said, "wait up, I'll give you a hand, that ladder looks like it's a little heavy."

When Sam and Justin returned, they attached the ladder to the block and tackle rope. Rick pulled on the rope to carry the new ladder up to the tree house. Sam hurried up the extension ladder so he could grab the new ladder and install it on the platform in front of the door. "I have the ladder, Rick," Sam hollered down.

Sam untied the new ladder and hooked the metal arches into the two holes on the floor of the platform.

"HERE IT GOES!" Sam shouted with extreme excitement as the ladder unrolled towards the ground.

Everyone cheered. The ladder hung from the platform to just a foot above the ground. "What a perfect fit," Joey said.

"Justin, we still have one more important thing to finish." Rick said. "We need to paint the banner."

Rick asked Mom if he could have an old white sheet. When she handed Rick a twin size bed sheet, she asked, "What do you plan to do with it?"

"We're going to paint THE F.B.I. CLUB on it. We're going to use it as our banner," Rick explained. "Justin is going to sketch the letters on the fabric. We'll nail it to the garage wall to make it easier to work on. Not to worry, Mom, I don't think the black paint will go through the sheet."

Justin and Rick took the white sheet and headed to the garage. After hanging and stretching the sheet against the wall, Justin began drawing each letter; Rick went behind him and brushed each letter in with black paint.

THE F.B.I. CLUB
THE FAMOUS BOY INVESTIGATORS CLUB

"That didn't take long," Justin remarked. "Now, I wonder how we're going to hang our banner on the club house."

"Let's ask Mr. Davis before he leaves," Rick suggested. After Justin and Rick talked with Mr. Davis about the banner, they knew exactly what to do.

"When the sheet dries," Mr. Davis said, "I'll help you attach ten aluminum grommets on one side of the sheet. Then you can thread a rope through those grommets."

When the sheet was dry, all the boys carried the banner to Mr. Davis. He attached the grommets using a tool from his truck. Then they threaded the rope through, and he showed everyone how to unfurl the banner so it would fly straight.

chapter four

MAKING PLANS

After church on Sunday, Rick called the members of the F.B.I. Club to come to their newly constructed club house at seven o'clock that evening, so they could make plans for their newest investigation. At six-forty-five, Rick climbed up the ladder to wait for the other members. Joey followed Rick up the tree house ladder. "Joey, you can't stay here. This meeting is for members only!" Rick said firmly.

Joey begged, "But Rick, they're my friends, too. Besides, you know I want to be a Junior Investigator, too."

"Remember your ketchup incident? We don't have time for your tricks. This is serious business," Rick answered.

"Rick," Joey pleaded, "please let me just sit in the meeting. I promise to behave and be quiet!"

Rick decided, "All right, you can stay as long as you keep your promise and behave."

"Thanks, Rick!" Joey exclaimed with delight, "I won't let you down this time!"

When Sam and Pete arrived, they climbed the ladder to the tree house. "Where is everybody?" Pete asked.

"Let's wait for a few minutes," Sam suggested. "It's still early yet."

"Garth has a paper route, but he's usually on time," Rick remarked. "Oh, by the way, Pete, since the F.B.I. Club House is now official, would you please do the honor of hanging the banner out? Now, everyone will know that we're in business! That way, the other guys in the neighborhood will see that we're having a meeting."

"Right! Roger! Okay!" Pete replied, as he unfurled the F.B.I. Club banner. He put the pole in the bracket mounted beside the front door.

Garth and Justin arrived quickly, skidding to a stop at the bottom of the old oak tree. "Dillon is right behind us. I saw him turning onto Spring Street," Garth said. "Here we are! We're not late, are we?"

"Are we going to investigate a crime tonight?" Justin asked, as he and Garth climbed the ladder to the tree house.

"I'm ready to call the meeting to order, but for some unknown reason Dillon always seems to be late," Rick said with a sigh.

"You know his dad always finds something for him to do at the last minute," Justin remarked.

Dillon arrived suddenly. He hit the brakes sharply on his bike, leaving a cloud of dust engulfing him, and quickly scampered up the ladder. "Sorry to be late, guys. Did I miss anything?"

"No, not yet," Rick said. "Okay, I am glad to see everyone is finally here. Is there any old business to discuss?"

Sam stood up and said, "Yes, I have some old business. We need to send thank-you notes to everyone who contributed money, soda cans, and materials for our club house because without their help, this tree house would never have happened."

"Rick, since you are president of the F.B.I. Club," Justin said, "you should be the one to write the thank-you notes. Then we can all sign them at our next meeting."

"I second that motion," Pete said. "Rick has good grades in English anyway. He could write personal thank-you notes instead of just buying someone else's words on a card."

Rick said, "All in favor of me writing the thank-you notes say yea."

There was a chorus of yeas.

"Motion carried," Rick said. "It will be an easy job since I kept a record of the people who helped us. Sam, will you help me with the envelopes? You get good grades in handwriting." "Yes, Rick," Sam replied, "I don't mind addressing the envelopes if you will give me a copy of your list of the names and addresses. Do we have enough money left to buy stamps?"

"Yes," Rick replied, as he opened the record book. "There are five dollars and thirty-five cents left. I think that will be enough. Anyway, if we run out of stamps, we can always hand-deliver them."

"I would like to know when we are going to solve more crimes. Do you have a plan for solving crimes?" Justin asked, impatiently. "I hope we're going to catch some thugs, robbers, or gangs. We don't want them giving our town a bad name."

"That's for new business," Rick replied, "but, yes, I do. I have a plan that I want to discuss." He closed the record book. "Is there any more old business?" After a brief pause, Rick continued, but the boys had started talking and no one seemed to be listening to him. Rick banged the gavel on the picnic table to get everyone's attention. "All right, let's get on with the new business," Rick said, as he tried to get control of the meeting. Everyone was talking at once. Rick banged the gavel on the picnic table again. "Let's have order! Everyone can speak their piece, but we have to do it in an orderly manner."

"We can start with surveillance," Garth said. "We don't need a lot of electronic equipment, just a pair of binoculars. My dad bought a pair of night-vision binoculars for checking his job sites at night. I think he might let us use them. I'll ask him tonight."

"Thanks, Garth," Rick said, as he wrote down Garth's suggestion.

"I think we need a place to hide our bikes when we see a crime going on," Dillon suggested. "We can't just lay them on the ground or stand them up. That might get us in trouble because the gangsters would know that there are kids hanging around. What do you think?"

"Well," Sam remarked, "I suggest that we either put the bikes behind some bushes or behind a house across the street from the break-in. No one would be the wiser."

"My Dad told me about the many house break-ins around some of the neighborhoods where he has customers," Dillon related. "The police have asked him to keep his eyes open for strangers driving by or stopping at homes when the people are away. The police can't seem to catch them in the act of robbing. When the criminals see the police cruisers, they just hide until the coast is clear. Then, they go on with their devious work. Wouldn't it be cool if we could catch them ourselves?"

"Yes," Sam said, "that would be great! We need to keep our investigative business going. What we really need is a map of Mayfield and the surrounding areas."

"I think it would be a great idea to ride over to Elm Drive. I've heard there are some gangs that are breaking into houses over there. Since the police patrol can't seem to catch them in the act of robbing, maybe we can. We just need some tips on how to catch them," Justin stated.

"My uncle was in the army and he got a pair of night-vision binoculars," Garth said. "If my dad won't lend me his night-vision binoculars, I'll bet my uncle would let us use his, that way we could also do surveillance in the dark."

"I heard there are a lot of break-ins going on over on Pine Avenue," Pete said. ""We need to investigate that area, too."

"Dillon, can you ask your dad for a map of the city?" Sam asked. "We can tack the map on the wall right here beside the door."

"Yes," Dillon answered. "I'm sure he would give me one of his maps. I'll ask him tonight."

"I can bring some colored pins," Pete said. "Red to mark the unsolved crimes, green for the ones that are solved, and yellow for the ones that we have under surveillance."

"We need to find a way to keep in touch with everybody. Does anyone have a suggestion?" Justin asked.

"I have a suggestion," Dillon said. "We need to borrow cell phones from our families so we can keep in touch with each other."

"That's a great idea," Rick said. "Let's all bring them when we go out investigating."

"Okay," Garth said. "What can I do? Is there anything I can bring?"

Sam replied, "Oh, yes, I know something very important. Garth, you can bring pocket notebooks for everyone. Then we can write down the streets that we're going to patrol each time we go out. That way we can keep track of what we're doing."

"Sounds like a good idea to me," Garth remarked. "I can handle that problem."

"Let's adjourn the meeting," Rick suggested, "so we can get some things done. Come back Friday after supper and we'll finish our plans."

"Let's adjourn!" they all shouted. Sam, Pete, Justin, and Garth went down the ladder. Rick's mom called up to the club house to say, "It's time for you boys to get your chores done."

"We're coming, Mom," Rick said, as Joey and Dillon scampered down the ladder.

*****

The next day, Rick went to the library to look through back-issues of the local newspaper. He made notes of the crimes that had occurred during the past three months. He wrote down the names of the streets and the details of the criminal acts. He also noted the status of the crimes, solved or unsolved. There were even some articles about a reported kidnapping: a child had been taken from the parking lot at the mall, and the kidnappers had not yet been apprehended. No further information about the child was available, and it was unknown whether the child was alive or not. Rick made a note to ask his dad for an update, so he could keep his records current. Research was always very interesting for Rick. He enjoyed compiling data and facts.

After supper on Friday, Dillon and Pete rode their bikes to the bottom of the oak tree. "Here we are, Rick! What's up?

Are we going to investigate a crime tonight?" Dillon asked, excitedly.

"Yes, Dillon, as soon as we finish making our plans, we will go out to investigate break-ins."

"We brought our sleeping bags, flashlights, and clean clothes for tomorrow," Pete chimed in. "I'll put them in the bucket. Rick, will you pull the bucket up with my sleeping bag and clothes?"

"Sure thing, buddy!" Rick answered excitedly. He was proud to be the President if the F.B.I. Club. "Did you bring any chips or something like that to munch on?" Then he pulled the rope through the block and tackle. He kept his eye on the bucket to make sure he didn't pull it too fast. He did not want the bucket to tip on the way up to the club house.

"Sure I did," Dillon said proudly, "and lots of sodas, too."

"Great! I'll bring the refreshments next time," Pete said. "I'll bring my favorite munchies, too. I think you'll like them. We can take turns bringing the snacks."

Justin rode up on his bike. "I'm ready to go out and hunt for clues," he said, with excitement in his voice.

"Are we going to catch robbers tonight?" Pete asked again.

"I certainly hope so," Rick answered. "I spent most of Monday afternoon at the library researching the crimes over the past three months. I found that when homeowners were away on vacation, they returned to find their houses broken into and robbed. Maybe we can discover some clues to help catch the burglars."

"My mom knows a lady over in Westhaven whose house was broken into while she was in the hospital. Her house was a mess when she got home. Luckily, she didn't have any valuables lying around for the thieves to take, but it was still upsetting," Dillon said.

"Oh, Sam called to say he couldn't come over this weekend," Justin said. "He is going camping in the mountains, and Garth is going with him, too."

"Too bad," Rick said. "They're going to miss some important investigations."

"Did you guys borrow a cell phone from your parents?" Rick asked. "We have cases to solve. We need to be prepared. Communication is the name of the game."

Mom called up from the bottom of the ladder and asked, "Rick, would you please take Joey with you? He has grown up a lot since our chat."

"All right, Mom," Rick said with a sigh. "Remember to tell him that this is for real! This is his last chance!"

Joey climbed the ladder shouting, "I'll be good! I promise. Mom even said I could use her tiny cell phone. See, I have it here in my jacket pocket!"

"Joey," Rick said sternly, "sit down and pay attention."

"I have my cell phone, too," Dillon said. "I even brought my walkie-talkies so we can keep in touch in case the cell phones don't work. Rick, do you want to keep one of the walkie-talkies and I'll keep the other one with me?"

"Sounds like a good idea to me," Rick answered. "Let's rehearse our phone numbers. Mine is 555-3337. Justin, what's yours?"

"It's 555-1728," Justin replied proudly. "I wrote your number in my little notebook. Dillon, what's yours? I want to write it in my notebook, too."

"It's 555-1677," Dillon said, as he wrote the numbers on the back of the comic book he was reading. "Garth didn't give me a notebook yet."

"Pete, what's yours?" Rick asked, as he was making his list of the cell phone numbers.

"It's 555-2157, Pete replied.

"Joey, what's yours?" Rick asked.

"Um, it's 555-77... The numbers are all worn off, I can barely read them," Joey said. "This is Mom's old cell phone."

"Joey, you'd better turn the cell phone on to be sure that it works," Rick suggested.

Joey began pushing buttons, but the phone would not come on. "Rick, the phone won't turn on. I think the battery's dead."

"Justin, you'd better give Joey the other walkie-talkie, just in case of an emergency. Joey, have you been writing down the cell phone numbers?" Rick asked.

"No," Joey replied, "I don't have any paper and I don't have a pencil either. I guess I should have been better prepared."

"Joey would lose his head if it wasn't connected to his shoulders," Rick snorted.

"Let's get going and ride our bikes around the neighborhood to see what's up," Justin suggested.

"Good!" Dillon said. "Let's go!"

The boys climbed down the ladder and mounted their bikes, preparing to ride off for a new investigation. Rick turned to look for Joey. "Where's Joey?"

"I saw him run into the house," Pete said. "He shouldn't be long."

When Joey came out of the house, Rick walked over to Joey and put a hand on his shoulder. "Joey, I don't think you should go out with us. You are not prepared. Something bad might happen to you. If you get yourself in trouble, Mom and Dad will blame me."

"I promise to be good," Joey pleaded. "Besides, I went back in the house and got a piece of paper and a pencil too. I even wrote down your cell phone number. I'll write down everyone else's phone numbers, too."

"All right, but this is the last time. You had better listen to me and stay out of trouble," Rick said, lovingly but sternly.

As the boys were preparing to leave, Dillon's dad, Mr. Notz, drove up in his station wagon beside the boys standing in Rick's driveway. "Here is the map for you to nail on the clubhouse wall. I also cut another map into sections for you to take with you during your investigations," Mr. Notz explained. "I think these maps will be a great help to you. I marked the areas where the break-ins have happened. Although my customers asked me to keep an eye on their property when they were away, the burglars got in anyway. Good luck with your investigations, boys. I'm sorry to tell you that I'm going to take Sam and Garth to the mountains for the weekend. Mr. Byrum is not feeling very well, so I volunteered to take the boys. I hope you won't be too disappointed. The map will be a help to you."

"That's okay. Mr. Notz, I understand. Thanks for the maps." Then Rick said to Sam, who was sitting in the back seat, "Sorry, Sam, that you can't ride with us, but the map sections will really help. We'll concentrate on the areas that Mr. Notz marked." Rick waved to Sam and Garth. "See you later, alligator."

Returning to his friends with the maps, Rick said with authority, "Okay, guys, let's patrol only the section that covers Sycamore Drive. We need to get some concrete clues about these crooks." After studying the map, Rick said, "Let's ride down Elm Drive, over to Maple and up Sycamore Drive. We can look for robbers there." Rick brought out his research notebook on break-ins.

"If we see a house where no one is home, we can hide our bikes and wait to see what happens," Justin said. He wrote the names of the streets in his notebook and checked the map to make sure he was correct.

"We'll spread out far enough so that all sides of the house can be seen," Rick said. "If you see something suspicious, we'll make detailed notes of what and who we see. I will be the one to call the police, but only after we get enough information. We must keep our eyes open; surely we will find something."

"Yeah," Joey said excitedly. "We need to find out if they have a car or truck and write down the license number. That way we can get more clues as to who the burglars are. They might even have a getaway car hidden somewhere."

Dillon shouted eagerly, "I hope we find something! My friend lives on Elm Drive. It's a nice neighborhood. Jake sometimes gets off the bus at my house and his dad picks him up after work. I don't think burglars would try anything over there."

"I only hope we can sleep after this adventure tonight," Joey said. "I don't want to get scarified again." The boys laughed as they prepared to begin their new investigation.

Stillness fell over the neighborhood as night finally arrived. The boys rode their bikes up Elm Drive. Their cell phones were clipped to their belts. They had flashlights mounted on their helmets, as well as lights on the fronts of their bikes. Joey had his walkie-talkie clipped to his belt in the back so that the antenna went up the back of his jacket. He didn't want it to get in the way of riding his bike.

The night was eerie. Darkness was deep except for the lights on their bikes and their helmets to light the way. Sometimes the moon would peek through the clouds, but only for a minute or two. They continued to ride from street to street: first, down Elm Drive, then across the Seventh Street Bridge. They rode slowly, checking out the houses on both sides of the street. Everything looked in order.

"Let's ride over to Maple Drive," Dillon suggested. "The streetlights will make it easier for us to see. It's just too dark over here."

I'm scared," Justin remarked nervously. "I agree with Dillon. It's very dark out here. What if a gang comes along? I heard that a gang broke into the Wilson Elementary School a couple of weeks ago. They are dangerous. They could be that teenage gang who doesn't like school and would probably turn the place upside-down. They might even be bigger than us, and then what would we do? Besides, we don't know enough about them to know where their turf is."

"There's nothing to worry about," Pete said. "I don't see anything wrong here. Let's ride over to Glenshaw where the gangs are known to hang out. They wouldn't bother us because we are just kids out for a joy ride."

"Well, I'm scared too," Dillon said, as he looked around in the darkness. "We shouldn't go over to Glenshaw. It's too dark. Let's go over to Maple Drive. I think it's safer. We must find some clues to help the police."

They rounded the corner of Maple Drive. The streetlights had a strange glow. The street was a little brighter. They rode slowly down the street, checking for clues on both sides. Suddenly, the moon peeked through the clouds. It cast a strong beam of light straight down on Maple Drive.

Pete signaled a halt. "Look at that white house across the street. It looks like the front door window is broken. I see a light in the window. Does anybody know who lives there?"

"Yes, Pete," Justin replied. "My mother's friend Mrs. Bennett lives there. She and my mom go to church together because Mrs. Bennett doesn't drive."

"Pete," Rick asked, "will you call your mom and see if she knows anything about Mrs. Bennett? You can let her know that we're going to investigate the broken door."

"Okay, Rick," Pete answered, "I'll call my mom right now." In a few minutes, Pete whispered to Rick that his mom's phone was busy. "I guess I'll call her back in a couple of minutes," he murmured.

"Maybe we need to investigate right away. We might find a clue to catch the robbers," Justin said, his voice shaking with fear.

"Keep calm, Justin," Rick whispered. "Let's put our bikes behind that big spruce tree. We can creep over there onto Mrs. Bennett's front porch and check out the situation. Does anybody know if Mrs. Bennett has gone away for the weekend?"

"Let me call my mom again," Pete said quietly. "She drives Mrs. Bennett to church. She would be the one to know."

"Good!" Rick replied softly, "but we still need to investigate the front door. Let's go! Pete, you can catch up with us when you get an answer from your mom."

Rick, Joey, Pete, and Justin crept across the street as silently as possible. They noticed the front door was slightly open. The wood near the door lock was splintered. Pieces of wood and glass covered the doormat. Joey was the first one to reach the door. He suddenly stopped, tilted his head and listened intently for clues. He began to shiver with fear and said, "I hear a moan. We better call 911!"

"We need to go in to see if there's anything we can do to help," Rick urged, "I know we were only allowed to do surveillance, but someone's life may be in danger!"

"Let's investigate further before we call 911," Pete said. "I'll creep around the side of the house to see if there's any activity. The robbers could still be in the house, and they could catch us. Then we would really be in a pickle."

"Move back, Joey," Rick said. "Stay out here and be very quiet, and when it's time, I'll call the police and tell them where we are. In the meantime, write down this house number on Maple Drive. We might need an ambulance if someone is hurt inside. Now, let me peep into the broken door," he said as he exchanged places with Joey.

"What do you see?" Justin whispered nervously. "Are the crooks gone? Can you see anything? What's up?"

"Shush! Be quiet, Justin," Rick instructed, as he pushed on the door. It opened easily. There on the floor lay Mrs. Bennett. She was tied up in ropes to a chair that had fallen over. Her head was bleeding and she was moaning.

"Are you okay? Who did this terrible thing to you?" Rick asked, with a shocked expression on his face. He had never seen a sight such as this in his life.

"I can't believe this has happened to me," Mrs. Bennett said. "I just came back from my vacation. They were already inside the house when I came in the back door. Please sit me up."

Rick jumped into action, and called to Justin to help. Together they struggled to lift Mrs. Bennett and the chair into an upright position while asking her for clues.

"I don't know who they were. They wore masks over their faces but I did see the backs of their jackets. They had a big white rat or a squirrel painted on the back of their black leather jackets. They were so mean to me. They wanted all of my money. When I told them I didn't have any, they tore my bedroom apart. They said I should have some money and jewelry. Then one of those thieves tied me up like this and hit me on the head. I didn't know what they took, but they left in a hurry," Mrs. Bennett said in a whisper. "Are the police coming, yet? My head hurts!"

"Hold on, I'll call 911 and I'll give them your address and directions," Rick told her. While dialing his cell phone, Rick ran to the front door. "Here Joey, take this flashlight so you can direct the ambulance to the side door. I think it is the easiest way to get to her."

In a few minutes, the sirens could be heard coming down Maple Drive. The red lights were flashing. As the rescue squad drove into the driveway, Joey directed the ambulance using his flashlight.

"Please hurry. She is hurt bad. She is even tied up with ropes," Dillon said, as he directed the attendants up to the living room.

"Okay, boys, we'll take it from here," the paramedic said, as he and his crew began to cut off the ropes. Soon they lifted Mrs. Bennett up and put her on a stretcher for a quick ride to the hospital.

Police Chief George Adams entered the robbery scene through the broken front door. He brought his photographer with him to take pictures of the crime scene. "Thanks, boys, you probably saved that woman's life. How did you know to come here?"

"We are the F.B.I. Club, the Famous Boy Investigators Club," Rick said proudly. "We were riding around the neighborhood checking to see if a crime was happening because of all the recent robberies. We thought we might find some clues."

"When we saw the broken door, we knew something was wrong so we investigated and that's when we found Mrs. Bennett," Joey interjected.

"That was very brave of you boys, but this is police work," Police Chief Adams said. "We will hunt for clues, apprehend the culprits, and take them off to jail. You must be careful because some of the gangs are vicious." Chief Adams then followed the photographer through the house.

The boys left quietly. They met at the big spruce tree to gather their bikes. They gave each other the "high five" for a successful investigation and saving Mrs. Bennett's life. They headed back to the F.B.I. club house.

"I'm hungry!" Dillon said. "I really worked up an appetite. I could eat a horse right now if I had one, but a peanut butter sandwich would be tastier."

"Me too!" added Joey.

"I could eat an elephant if I had a knife and fork," Pete said, as he and the boys pedaled their bikes across the Seventh Street Bridge. The cool air was coming off the river. It made them feel both sleepy and hungry as they pedaled to Rick's house.

"I'm so glad that we brought our sleeping bags to the club house," Justin said. "It won't take me very long to get to sleep."

The boys put their bikes beside the porch. They went into the kitchen for peanut butter and jelly sandwiches and large glasses of cold milk.

While they were in the kitchen, they heard the stairs squeak. "Who's down there?" Dad asked. Mom was close behind him. "We thought you were bandits or something. We had to investigate," Mom added.

"It's just Joey, me, Justin, Pete, and Dillon, Dad," Rick told him, "We have just come back from our investigation. We found a broken windowpane in Mrs. Bennett's front door. We found Mrs. Bennett tied up to a chair with ropes. The chair had been knocked over. She was hurt bad. I'm sure that we saved Mrs. Bennett's life. And we found a clue as to who had broken into her house and hurt her."

"What happened?" Dad asked.

"The moon shone on the broken window pane on her front door," Rick went on, "so we crept across the street to investigate. That's when we heard her moan and cry for help."

Pete continued, "She was lying on the floor, and her head was bleeding. The thieves tied her to a chair with ropes and knocked her chair over. She said they hit her because she told them she didn't have any money. She told us that they wore black leather jackets with a rat or squirrel painted on the back."

"What did you do to help Mrs. Bennett?" Dad asked, as if he was the detective on the case.

"I called 911," Rick reported, "and told the officer the address. I also asked for an ambulance because Mrs. Bennett was hurt pretty bad."

"Yeah," Joey continued, "and I used my flashlight to show the ambulance where to find the driveway close to the house."

"That was very brave of you, Joey," Dad said. "However, you were close to danger. There could have been thugs hiding outside waiting to jump on you. They could have hurt you, too."

"You're right, Dad," Joey said, with downcast eyes. "I understand, but I want to be a Junior Investigator so badly that I wanted to help in any way to show how responsible I am!"

Then a thought came to Mr. Spencer. "Your clues lead me to believe that this might be the River Rat Gang from over in Glenshaw. They are a mean gang of thieves. We just can't seem to catch them in the act of breaking and entering. We have arrested them several times for suspicion of robbery, but we didn't find the loot. So we had to release them. They must have a secure hiding place somewhere."

"When I did the research at the library last week, there was a big article about that gang," Rick said, as he checked his notes from the newspaper article.

"You boys better let the police do their job," Mom said, as she walked into the dining room and put out a plate of her famous chocolate brownies. "Boys, bring your sandwiches and milk in here. Then we can all have dessert together. I don't want you boys to get hurt with this detective business."

The junior investigators shared all the details of their adventure. Finally, the boys calmed down. Mrs. Spencer asked, "Do all of you boys have your sleeping bags in the club house?"

"I haven't brought mine yet," Dillon said, "but I can sleep on the floor. It's no big deal."

"Let me get a couple of quilts. The floor is too hard for you to sleep properly," Mrs. Spencer said, as she left the room.

After finishing their snack, they cleaned up the dining room table and washed their hands and faces. Rick, Joey, Justin, Dillon, and Pete climbed the ladder and slid into their sleeping bags. Dillon got comfortable on the soft quilt and warm blanket. In the wink of an eye, they were sound asleep.

When the rays of sunlight came streaming in the window, the boys yawned, stretched, and decided to get ready for the new day. They were excited and curious as to what this new day had in store for them.

They climbed down the ladder for a hearty breakfast at Rick's house. While they enjoyed scrambled eggs, bacon, and a large glass of cold milk, they discussed how they were going to solve more crimes. They opened the morning newspaper and immediately turned to the section where the police report was listed. They quickly located the report of the break-in at 621 Maple Drive. "Home invasion, homeowner attacked and robbed. Forced entry was made through the front door. Money and jewelry were taken."

"Those thieves don't want to quit," stated Dillon. "This article says that homes in the Meadowlands subdivision are being targeted. Houses are being broken into when the owners are on vacation or at the hospital. That's how the crooks decide whom to rob and hope to get away with it. They don't have a neighborhood crime watch program set up."

"We can help if we get a peek at the gang, or if we can write down a description of the getaway car or a license number," Rick said. "We can go out again tonight and see if we can do something to help the community."

"Dillon and I are going home now," Justin said. "We'll be back to help you search for the robbers. See you later."

"Goodbye," Pete said. "I'll be back again tonight after supper." They jumped on their bikes and rode off toward their homes.

As evening turned into night, the five boys met up at Rick's house. First they rode their bikes up Trade Street. Joey had his walkie-talkie fastened to his belt. The antenna was safely hidden under his jacket. He didn't want the wire to interfere with his riding his bike. He was thinking ahead in case he had to make a quick getaway.

They rode their bikes slowly so they could get a better look at the houses. It became even more difficult to see as the clouds covered the moon. The only light remaining came from their helmets and the headlights on their bikes.

All of a sudden, Justin pulled in front of the others and said, "Look at that two-story house over there. I saw a flashlight going on and off through the side window."

"Write down that address," Rick ordered. "Then let's ride around the back of the house to see if they have a broken window or door. That might give us another clue." Rick and the others rode down the alley near the back of the house. They saw an old black van parked right behind the house. The boys hid safely behind the house to survey the situation.

"Joey, you are the smallest one. Can you crawl up close enough to get the license number of the van?" Rick asked.

"Sure thing, Rick, I can do that!" Joey replied bravely, as he crawled towards the back of the black van. His eyes got as big as saucers. He began to tremble. Sweat began to drip into his eyes. He eyes were fixed on the painting of a big white rat on the back of the black van. The vehicle was dusty and dirty. At first, it was hard to read. He crawled closer until he could read the words "River Rat Pest Control." Joey was so nervous he tore a hole in the white paper as he wrote down the license number. The paper dropped on the ground and was lost in the darkness.

He quickly decided to write the license number on the back of his hand. Finally, he crawled back to his waiting friends. "I got it! Here it is!" Joey said, shaking all over. "I wrote the license number on the back of my hand." He was really scared out of his wits.

"Hey guys, there was a big ugly rat painted on the back of the van. I think it said River Rat Pest Control. Could that be the River Rat Gang?" Joey whispered.

Rick patted Joey on the back, and said, "It could be. Good job, Joey! Now, let's ride back across the street and keep surveillance on the house."

"Right! Roger! Okay!" The Junior Investigators whispered, as they pushed their bikes out of the alley. They crossed the street and crawled behind the bushes to keep an eye on the house.

"If it is the River Rat Gang, we know they will be vicious," Pete warned.

"I see a flashlight going on and off again. I also see movement in the front room," Justin whispered to Rick. "I think we need to call the police before they get away with everything."

Rick agreed and dialed 911. He told the operator that they were at 557 Elm Avenue. He explained that a house was being robbed across the street at 558 Elm Avenue. "It looks like there are several people moving inside the house. I'll keep my night-vision binoculars on the house until the police arrive."

Rick crawled around each of the other investigators. "Stay under cover until the police get here so that we won't get hurt," Rick reminded them. "Just keep calm and keep your eyes open."

Within five minutes, the police cars came down Elm Avenue. They turned off their headlights and drove into the alley. Unmarked police cars took up positions at each end of the alley.

Chief Adams got out of the car. He whispered to Rick, "What did you see?"

"There's an old, dirty black van in the alley. It has a white rat painted on the door. Joey said it reads: River Rat Pest Control. We also noticed a flashlight going on and off through the first floor of that two story house across the street. It looks suspicious. That's why I called you. We didn't go onto the property to investigate. It looked too scary for us."

"That was a wise decision, son. If it is the River Rat Gang, then I know they are dangerous. I'll take over from here," Chief Adams said.

"I've kept surveillance on the house with my night-vision binoculars. Do you want to use them?" Justin offered.

"Thanks, don't mind if I do," Chief Adams said, as he took the night-vision binoculars from Justin.

Chief Adams spoke into his radio to his fellow officers. "Maintain your position until further orders." Chief Adams cautioned, "I can tell the robbers are still in the house. Stay low, boys. I have the situation under control." Then he spoke into a megaphone. "All right! This is the police! Everyone come out with your hands up!! Don't try anything stupid. The house is surrounded."

"Come and get us, coppers!" the robbers yelled through the door. "We ain't coming out. You'll have to come and get us." Suddenly a bullet whizzed by, close to the Police Chief's ear.

"Now that makes me very angry!" Chief Adams said to himself, as he brushed the heat of the bullet away from his ear. "Enough is enough," he called into the megaphone. "This is your final warning. Now, at the count of five, we're going to come in and get you. So, I suggest that you come out peaceably. One... Two... Three... Four... Five!" Chief Adams ordered his marksman to load up a tear gas canister and shoot it into the front room through the broken window. There was no response. "All right, I guess you want to come out in a hurry," he called. A loud explosion was heard. In a few minutes, smoke billowed out the broken window and the door. The River Rat Gang came out coughing and choking.

"Don't shoot! We give up," the thugs said, as they held their hands above their heads.

Chief Adams handcuffed the robbers and put them in the police car. His deputy came around the side of the house with another criminal in handcuffs. "This one thought he was going to leave in the van. He was mistaken! I called for a city tow truck to take the van in for evidence. It might even be holding some of the loot that was stolen."

Police Chief Adams came across the street and thanked the boys for their help. "I can see that you boys will make great investigators when you grow up. It's good to know that one of the worst gangs is now off the street," said Police Chief Adams.

"I'll bet they're the culprits who tied up and robbed poor Mrs. Bennett," Justin said. "She gave a description of their jackets!"

"I hope the judge locks them up for a long time," Dillon added.

"Well, we've done our duty. I'll take the robbers to the police station and see if I find out anything else about them," Police Chief Adams said.

The boys jumped high in the air, giving each other the 'high five' for a successful investigation and the capture of the River Rat Gang. Then, Rick, Joey, Pete, Justin and Dillon returned to their bikes and headed for home. The River Rat Gang was out of business.

"I'm hungry," Pete said, as he mounted his bike. "I could eat a giraffe right now, if only I had one."

"I could eat anything that wasn't nailed down," Dillon added, as he popped a lifesaver in his mouth. His mouth was so dry, it felt like a desert.

"I agree," Rick said. "The investigation business is very tiring, but we will get better as we help solve crimes in the city."

The boys reached the club house and climbed the ladder. As they prepared to slide into their sleeping bags, Joey pulled out a box of Apple Jacks. He passed the box around. Everyone took a handful.

"Are there drinks?" Dillon asked. "You can't eat Apple Jacks without milk."

"Hold your horses!" Joey replied. "I put some chocolate milk in the cooler before we left so it would be cold when we got back. How's that for drinks?"

"Great! Pass it around. Do you have bowls, too?" Garth asked, as he laughed at the handful of Apple Jacks in his hand. He had nowhere to pour the chocolate milk.

"I didn't think about that," Joey apologized. "I guess I'll have to go down to the kitchen and get the bowls. Don't go to sleep before I get back, okay?"

"Sure thing," Justin said. "I'll eat my Apple Jacks so I can pull the bucket up when you get back with everything."

"You'd better send up some wet wash rags and paper towels too, along with the bowls. and maybe bring some white milk, too," Pete said.

"Right! Roger! Okay!" Joey said, as he climbed down the ladder.

Dillon hollered down to the ground, "Joey, we need spoons, too. Don't forget the spoons."

Everyone laughed and giggled at Garth's remark. They knew Joey was trying hard to please everyone, but in his excitement, he kept forgetting something.

In a few minutes, the bucket was filled with the makings for a good night snack. Sleep followed as the five Junior Investigators drifted off to dream, reliving the excitement of the adventure.

chapter five

A DAY AT THE CARNIVAL

There was a lot of excitement throughout the community as the news spread concerning Mrs. Bennett's rescue. The boys of the F.B.I. club were asked at school by all their friends to tell them the details of their adventure.

A few weeks later, Pete and Joey decided to ride their bikes toward the farmland beyond their neighborhood. As they rode, they stopped and read a poster on a telephone pole. They soon discovered the Annual Community Carnival setting up at the fairgrounds. They realized that it was to open that very evening. Rick, Sam, Justin, Dillon and Garth appeared, approaching the fairgrounds from the opposite direction. They waved Hello to Pete and Joey. "What are you two guys up to?" Sam asked, as he watched the trucks unloading in the center of the fairgrounds.

"We just came to see what's happening. Do you want to come with us?" Pete asked.

"That looks good to me," Sam said. "Maybe we can get a job here. All they can say is No!"

They rode into the fairgrounds to watch some carnival workers begin to put up the rides. Other workers stacked the booths and tents to be put up later. It was exciting to watch. There were two elephants, a mother and her baby. They carried the tent poles and put them in a pile where they were directed. First, the workers unfolded the big circus tent. Then the men erected the four corner poles. Next, they opened the tent door for the mother elephant to bring in the two big center poles, carrying them with her trunk. She brought in one center pole, and returned to get the other one. Finally, the mother elephant and the trainer entered the big tent. "UP! UP! UP!" called the trainer. The center of the tent went up. The workers anchored the remaining poles in place with ropes. When the mother elephant came out of the tent with her trainer, she was given a handful of peanuts for a job well done. The boys were mystified as to how that elephant could put up those poles so straight.

"Don't be silly," Dillon remarked. "The elephants only carried the poles into the tent, and the trainer and a worker put the poles up."

Next, the roller coaster, kiddy rides, and Tilt-a-Whirl were put together. The men put each spoke together and put colored seats between the spokes. They anchored them together. The boys watched as each seat was set in place on the Ferris wheel. First, a red seat was put on the bottom of the wheel, then a blue one and then a yellow seat. The men crawled around the spokes just like monkeys. At last, the Ferris wheel was made into a complete circle and all of the seats were in place. The men crawled down from the spokes and turned on the motor to check that it was safe to ride. Around and around it went. Then it stopped at each seat to be inspected again. Soon the men left the Ferris wheel and went over to put the merry-go-round together.

"Isn't this amazing?" Justin remarked. "I never knew it took that much work to put a carnival together. I sure would like to learn how to do it."

As the boys were admiring the work of the carnival workers, a voice brought them back to reality.

"Do you boys want a job?" the carnival Barker asked. "We have booths for the stuffed animals that need to be put together. We have tents and booths for the ring toss, milk bottles, and penny pitch. All of the prizes need to be hung at every booth and every game. Are you interested? The roustabouts are pretty busy doing the heavy work."

"What's a roustabout?" Dillon asked, wondering at the strange-sounding word.

"They're the carnival workers who make sure the tent poles are secured, the rides are safe, and every other odd job you could think of is done."

"Gee, guys," Joey said, "I never knew the workers had a job title. That must have been the roustabouts we saw putting the Ferris wheel together. I think I would like to be a roustabout when I grow up. You know I want to be a body builder, and what a way to use my muscles!"

Taking charge, Rick spoke up, "Yes, we want to work!" The boys shouted "Yes!" in unison. "Where do we start? What do you want us to do?" Rick asked. He was clearly the spokesman for the group.

"Are you ready to construct the booths for the games in the midway?" the Barker asked.

"Yes, we are," Rick quickly replied, "How much are you going to pay us?"

"We usually pay twenty dollars a day," the Barker replied.

"That's all right with us, as long as each of us gets twenty dollars a day," Rick clearly stated.

"It's a deal, boys. Let's shake on it." After each boy shook the Barker's hand, they listened carefully to his instructions.

"This job is really very easy. All of the boards are marked "a to a" or "b to b." You just need to match each of the letters together." They laid the boards for the first booth out on the ground. "The booth has three full tall sides, and the front is half as tall. The short side is the counter for the customers. The roof is just a large piece of canvas with hooks on all four sides. The roof goes on the upper boards. Unwrap the canvas and hook it on. When you put the bottom boards on, then it will be complete. Do you want me to show you how to put one of the booths together?" the Barker asked.

"No thank you, we are members of the F.B.I. Club, the Famous Boy Investigators Club," Rick said proudly. "We are experts at finding clues, so I feel certain that we will be able to construct the booths for you."

"That takes a load off of my mind," the Barker said. "I'll be back to check on your progress shortly."

"Let's get to work," Rick said. "After this, we'll know if we want to be roustabouts when we grow up. I don't think I would want to be one, but I think this job will be interesting anyway."

Rick and Sam cleared a spot on the grass between the tent stakes and the dirt. Pete looked down the row of stakes to see that they were all neatly in a line.

"If we all work together," Rick said, "we can have the booths up in no time at all."

"Sounds like a good idea to me," Pete said. "Just tell me what to do and I will follow orders."

"Count me in, too," Dillon chimed in. "What do you want Pete and me to do?"

"Unwrap the next booth and put it together. Let me know when you're finished," Rick instructed.

In a short time, the first booth was constructed. Joey noticed a heavy cord that was connected to the booth roof in the back. He pulled the cord. It ran on pulleys. "Gee, guys," Joey said, "we can stand right here and put the stuffed animals on that cord and it will go to the other end."

"Justin, help me carry these three 55-gallon drums inside this booth. You can stand on them," Sam said. "Then, one of you guys can unpack these boxes and hang the teddy bears and the larger animals on the cord. When that cord is filled with stuffed animals, then you can come over and help us with the next booth in the midway."

"I see some smaller boxes that need to be opened and put on display, too." Joey said. "They're marked Penny Pitch." He opened one of the boxes, which was full of glasses and saucers. "Yes, I think that one goes to the Penny Pitch." Joey, Dillon, and Pete put up the large booth for the Penny Pitch. They unfolded a square table. It didn't have any legs, so they looked around and found six concrete blocks and put the table on them.

The boys went about their assigned tasks. They set up the milk bottles on the overturned wash tub. They stopped to watch intently as the elephant and her baby carried the Tower of Strength to the center of the midway. After several hours, when all of the booths were completed and all the stuffed animals hung in place, they went looking for the Barker

In a few minutes, as they walked around the colorful Kiddy rides, they spotted the Barker. He came to the booth section on the midway to inspect the boys' work.

"That was a fine job you boys did," the Barker told the boys. "You did a great job of cleaning up the area, too."

"Do you have any other jobs for us to do?" Rick asked.

"Yes, there is something you can do," the Barker said. "The elephants need water and some hay. There are bales of hay in the truck parked near their shelter. Look for a broken bale and bring two big sections of clover hay put into their trough. There are two white five-gallon buckets. Take them to the spigot and only fill them half-full. They have a wash tub for water and we like to keep it full. Each of you boys take turns refreshing the elephants."

When that chore was completed, they walked to the Kiddy rides. The boys followed the roustabouts who assembled the platform for the Tower of Strength. When it was erected and leveled, the trainer brought the elephants over and put the Tower of Strength in the square hole where it was anchored in place. The Tower of Strength is a game that tests your strength using a large, heavy, wooden sledgehammer. A person who is strong enough can strike the pad with the sledgehammer hard enough to make the metal disk rise to the top and ring the gong loudly.

"Now that the Tower of Strength is up," Joey asked, "do you think they would let me have a couple of practice swings?"

The carnival Barker, wearing his black and white checkered vest and straw hat and carrying his golden cane, came by and told them what a good job they had done feeding and watering the elephants.

"Could I have a few practice swings at the Tower of Strength?" Joey asked hopefully. "My friend, Pete and I are pumping iron with our 2-pound dumbbells. I want to be a body builder when I grow up. The ancient Greek body builder, Atlas, is my hero. Can I give it a try?" he asked, without begging.

"Sure you can, if you can lift the sledgehammer off the floor," the Barker said laughingly, as he looked at Joey's skinny arms.

Joey stood in front of the Tower of Strength. He flexed his muscles. He picked up the heavy sledgehammer as far as he could and let it fall with all his might. The metal disk went a few feet up the tower, but fell back to the base. "Can I have one more try, please?" Joey pleaded.

The Barker laughed and said, "Sure, if you have any strength left."

Joey inhaled deeply, picked up the sledgehammer and swung. This time the disk went halfway up the tower. Joey reeled back in exhaustion, but happy that he was even able to swing the sledgehammer. It was so heavy. He flexed his muscles, wiped the sweat from his brow, adjusted his trousers and put his feet firmly on the platform. Then, he didn't know how, he got the sledgehammer over his head and rested it on his shoulders. He let go with all of the strength he had left in his body. "BONG!" The bell rang! Joey collapsed to the floor with amazement at the sound of the bell ringing.

"Well, I'll be a monkey's uncle!" the Barker said, in astonishment, "I didn't think you could do it!" Joey was lying flat on the platform with the sledgehammer beside him. He had the largest grin of any boy the Barker had ever seen.

Rick, Pete, Sam, Garth, Dillon and Justin jumped for joy, yelling, "Hip! Hip! Hurray! He did it! I can't believe it, but I saw it with my own eyes," the boys said to each other.

"Do you want a ride to the paymaster's wagon?" the animal trainer asked, as he brought the two elephants to the platform. "By the way, which one of those boys hit the gong?" the trainer asked the Barker.

"It was the littlest one. I don't know how he even got the sledge hammer off the platform, but in three swings he hit the gong."

The big elephant gave a loud trumpet as if to say "Good Show" for ringing the gong.

"We're on our way to the paymaster's wagon," the trainer said. "Do you boys want to ride on Bingo? She is one of the biggest elephants and enjoys carrying people on her back. That's her baby. His name is Black Jack. She is teaching him how to carry poles in his trunk."

"Yes, I would like a ride," Pete replied, with a yawn. "I worked very hard today unpacking and putting prizes in the booths."

"Me too," Sam said. "Rick and I have worked hard, too. I've never ridden on an elephant before. I think it would be great! Don't you think so, Rick?"

"I sure do," Rick replied. "That would put the icing on the cake for us, to end the day with an elephant ride."

Justin and Garth were so excited about the elephant ride. "Do you want to get on first, Pete?" Justin asked.

"No," Pete replied. "I want to watch everyone else get on before me. I want to bring up the rear."

The trainer put his cane on Bingo's trunk. She curled her trunk near the ground on command. "Put your foot on her trunk and grab hold of the rope harness. She will lift you up and put you on her back. Not to worry, she knows how to do it very well."

Each boy took his turn getting lifted high in the air and deposited on Bingo's back. When all of the boys were lifted, Black Jack, the baby elephant, took hold of his mother's tail and followed behind as she carried them to the paymaster's wagon to get their pay and collect their bikes.

"Bingo likes to be helpful," the trainer said. "Her son, Black Jack, is just learning to do chores and to help his mother."

All too soon, the elephant arrived at the paymaster's wagon. The trainer told the boys to slide down Bingo's trunk. "She likes it, and besides it is a wonderful ride." Black Jack stood still, waiting for the trainer to give him another command.

"This is the first time I ever rode an elephant," Rick said, gleefully.

"I thought I would get a nosebleed being so high in the air," Pete said. "I always get a nosebleed when I ride in an elevator."

Joey was so excited, he shouted, "I sure would like to ride on Bingo again!"

The Paymaster gave each boy twenty dollars for his day's work. "By the way, boys, here is a free admission ticket for each of you for all the rides for your help."

They slowly pedaled their bikes home. Once they arrived home, they took a bath, a nap, and ate a hearty supper. They had had an exciting day. They began to plan to have an exciting evening.

After supper, the boys rode their bikes to the Annual Community Carnival. They were so excited. They wanted to ride everything, including another ride on Bingo.

Justin suggested they ride the Ferris wheel first. "That way we can see all over the fairgrounds and decide what to ride next."

"I want to ride the swings next," Pete said. "Do you want to do that?"

"Remember," Rick cautioned, "we must stick together or we'll get lost in the crowd. We'll never find each other again. Make sure to put five dollars away for food before we go home. Listen up, Joey. Don't count your money while you're high up on the Ferris wheel."

On the Ferris wheel, they planned their next few rides. "Okay, let's ride the swings next," Rick said as they got off the Ferris wheel.

"I want to ride the roller coaster after that," Joey said. "I don't like the swings, but I'll ride them anyway. I hope I don't get sick."

When they got off the roller coaster, Dillon led the way to the Haunted House and the House of Mirrors. It was scary, but fun. They even rode the Tilt-a-Whirl. Next, the boys moved toward the midway booths of games and prizes. They paid their money to try to hit the milk bottles, and shoot at the moving targets. They threw the rings for the Ring Toss game. Sam won a prize, a large teddy bear wearing a Sponge Bob Square Pants T-shirt. "Gee, wasn't that great! I got all five rings over the pins. I couldn't do that this afternoon when I helped set the game up."

As they were walking around the midway, they heard some men and women call out. "My wallet is gone. It's been stolen!" Several women who were in line for refreshments screamed, "My wallet is missing from my purse. Call the police!"

Rick and Justin heard the shouts. "Let's go looking for those pickpockets. They have to be around here somewhere," Rick said. "Garth, you and Pete go to the right and check any strange behavior. Sam and Dillon, go to the left. Look carefully. Let's meet back here in fifteen minutes. Maybe we can find them."

Rick and Joey went to the concession stands and looked for suspicious persons.

Rick noticed four boys who were laughing and counting a lot of cash and change.

Joey whispered to Rick, "I just saw one of those boys throw a wallet in the trash can. What should we do?" he whispered nervously.

"Let's go over to a picnic table. You stay here and keep watch while I go for help," Rick instructed.

Rick went to the side show where he had last seen the Barker. "Thank goodness, you're still here," Rick said, almost out of breath. "We found four boys who look like they are pickpockets. I left Joey there to keep them under surveillance until I could get help. Will you come with me?"

"Yes, I will," the Barker replied. "I will get one of our security men to go with us." The Barker waved his cane high in the air, and a security guard came right over.

"What do you need, boss?" the security guard asked.

"This young man has spotted some pickpockets and we need to investigate it right away. Will you go with him?"

"Sure thing, son. Lead the way," the security guard replied.

When they got to the picnic table, Joey told all about the wallets being thrown in the trash can. "I saw them do it. I kept them under surveillance."

"Thanks boys, I'll take it from here," the security guard said. "We need more honest young men like you around here."

In a few minutes, the boys all met at their arranged meeting place. Rick told them how he and Joey had found the pickpockets and turned them over to the security guard.

"Now can we have some more fun?" Dillon asked.

As they were walking down the midway, they heard the Barker yelling to the people who were walking past, "Step right up! See the magician saw a woman in half. Watch some of his great illusions. Step right up! Fifty cents, one half of a dollar!" He spun his cane around and pointed it at the stage. "The show begins in five minutes. Step right up! Don't miss this show. See the lovely lady being sawed in half."

"Let's check our pockets," Pete said. "I hope we have enough money to see the lady cut in half. I wonder how he does it."

"It's just a trick," Garth said. "I saw her walking around this afternoon."

"Check your pockets," Rick said, "and don't forget that we have to keep five dollars aside so we can eat before we go home." The boys went to a picnic table and counted their money.

"I have fifty cents," Sam said. "Pete, what do you have?"

"I have thirty-five cents," said Pete. "I spent a lot on the game with the ducks swimming in the trough. I did win a prize. Look, I won an inflatable lizard. It will look good in my room."

"Joey, where's your money?" Rick demanded.

"I only have forty cents left," Joey replied. "Can you lend me a dine?"

"I need fifteen cents," Pete said. "Now, what are we going to do? I want to see the lady get cut in half too."

"Look in your pockets again," Sam said.

Just then, Joey spotted a shiny dime on the ground. "I can get in!" Joey shouted.

Rick, Joey, Sam, Justin and Garth stepped up to the Barker. "Here's our money, but I guess our friend can't get in because he only has thirty-five cents," said Rick.

"I'll take the thirty-five cents," the Barker said, "and you boys enjoy yourselves. It's the greatest show you'll ever see."

The boys went into the tent and took seats on the front row by the stage. "I really want to see that lady get sawed in half. Do you think the blood will get all over us?" Joey said excitedly.

"Don't be silly, Joey," Rick said. "It's just an illusion. He isn't really going to cut her in half. I don't know how he does it, but I think she's his wife or something."

Suddenly, the curtain opened, and the magician stepped out on the stage so close to the edge that he almost touched Joey. He pulled a colorful handkerchief out of his jacket pocket. He reached into his side pocket and pulled out another colorful handkerchief. Then he showed them to the crowd and tied the two corners into a knot. He stuffed them into his cupped hand, took a magic wand, and waved it over his hand that held the colorful handkerchiefs.

Joey watched intently. He was sure he could see what the magician was doing. "Look, Sam," Joey said. "He doesn't have anything in those handkerchiefs."

The magician said, "Abracadabra." He poked his magic wand into his fist. When he opened his hand, the handkerchiefs were gone, as if they had disappeared into outer space!

"Where did they go?" Pete asked in astonishment. "I was sure that I saw exactly what he did. This magician is good!"

The magician asked the audience if they knew where the handkerchiefs had gone. Several voices called out. "Up your sleeve!" "Inside your jacket!" Pete yelled out, "They're in your other hand. Let me see!"

"Young man in the front row," the magician said, "the one who said they were in my other hand. Will you come up on the stage, please?"

"What should I do?" Pete asked nervously.

"Go up there right now and see if you can find those handkerchiefs," Sam ordered.

"Be cool! Hurry and get up on the stage, I want to know where the handkerchiefs are too," Joey said excitedly.

Pete ran up the steps to the stage, trembling with fear. He stood beside the magician. His legs felt like rubber sticks, and his head was spinning. He didn't want the magician to make him disappear into thin air.

The magician asked his name and how old he was.

"My name is Pete Martinez and I'm eleven and one-half years old. Where did the handkerchiefs go? I was sure that I watched you closely," Pete replied nervously.

"Ahh," the magician replied, "they're right here." In one quick second, the magician pulled the knotted handkerchiefs from the back of Pete's jacket! When the magician rubbed the knots together, they came apart instantly. Pete started to leave the stage, but the magician asked him to wait. "I have one more thing to show you, and I know you have keen eyesight so watch carefully." He took the handkerchiefs again, stuffed them into his closed hand. He tapped the magic wand on his closed fist. "Abracadabra!" the magician said loudly. "Did you see that?" he asked Pete.

"Yes, I watched carefully. They're still in your closed fist," Pete said confidently.

The magician tapped again with his magic wand and said "Abracadabra!" When he opened his fist, a white dove struggled out of his hand and landed on Pete's head.

The audience went wild with laughter and clapped and clapped at how he could get a white dove out of two handkerchiefs and a closed fist.

"That's magic," the magician said. "You can take your seat now and watch carefully, because I'm going to saw my wife in half."

Pete ran off the stage and slid into his seat in the front row. "Did you see that?" he asked breathlessly. "Did you see how he pulled those handkerchiefs out of the back of my jacket?"

"Shush!" Sam whispered. "He's getting ready to put his wife in one of those black boxes. Look, she only has her head and feet sticking out."

The magician spun the black box around and around and put a curtain over the box. He pulled the curtain away and turned the box for all to see, and then with his handsaw, he began to saw the box in two. The lady only smiled. The magician used a silver blade to separate the box halves. He then spun both halves apart and showed them to the audience. The lady's feet wiggled out of the end of one of the boxes and her head bobbed out of the top of the other box. The magician spun the boxes again, put the two halves together, and pulled the blade out. He put the curtain around the two halves and said "Abracadabra!" Then the lady stepped out of the box and took a bow to the audience. Everyone was surprised that the lady was no longer in two pieces.

"I don't know how he did it, but it was spectacular," Sam said, shaking his head in astonishment.

Everyone clapped and cheered when the lady got out of the box and came to the edge of the stage with the magician. They took a bow together.

"I'm ready to go home now," Pete said. "That was quite an experience."

At last, since they had tired themselves out, they found a picnic table to sit and rest. Sam, Rick, Pete, Garth, and Justin found their five dollars they had put aside for hamburgers, cotton candy and large sodas. Joey had worked up such an appetite that he also wanted a funnel cake to share with his friends. He went through his pockets looking for the five dollars that Rick had told him to put aside. It wasn't there. He checked his jacket pockets and found two one-dollar bills.

"Gee, I only have two dollars left," Joey sighed. "I guess I'll have to go home hungry."

"You can pay for the funnel cake, Joey, and I'll share my soda with you," Rick said unhappily. Satisfied that they wouldn't let him starve to death; Joey went to the window and ordered a funnel cake and six forks.

After their stomachs were full of carnival food and their heads were whirling with the excitement of the day and the night, it was time to go home.

The boys slowly walked to their bikes. "Hey guys," Rick suddenly said, "we have a huge problem. How are we going to ride our bikes and hold these large animals on without us falling off? Does anybody have any suggestions?"

"I guess I had better call my brother Tom, and see if he will come down and pick us up," Pete suggested. "I'm tired and don't know if I have enough energy to pump my bike up the hill to go home. Does anybody have a quarter for the phone?"

"I don't," Justin said. "I spent all of my money at the games."

"I don't have any either," Sam said, "I had to win a prize for Justin. That was my last fifty cents."

"I don't have any either," Joey said, "because I bought the funnel cake with my last two dollars."

"Hey, Rick, do you have any money left?" Sam asked.

Rick went through his pockets and found a quarter. "Be careful, Sam, and don't misdial. It's the only one we have!

Tell him to hurry. We're tired, full of carnival food, plus we're broke."

"Hello, Tom," Pete said into the phone. "Can you come to the fairgrounds and pick me and my friends up? We're tired and have large stuffed animals we won at the carnival. We can't handle them on our bikes. We're also broke. Can you bring the truck? We have six bikes and the six of us. Thanks Tom, we'll be waiting at the entrance to the fairgrounds."

"Help is on the way," Pete told his friends, "Let's head for the entrance of the fairgrounds so he won't have to wait on us."

They struggled to push their bikes to the entrance, with a large shaggy dog barely balanced on the handlebars of Garth's bike. The large teddy bear wearing a Sponge Bob Square Pants T-shirt was being pushed on Sam's bike seat. Rick had a hard time keeping his sombrero barely balanced on his head while still being able to see where he was going. Pete put his Harley Davidson flag on the display clamp beside the red triangular flag that fluttered behind the seat of his bike. Joey attached his inflatable lizard flying from the back of his bike. Justin had his Huggy Monkey tied around his waist. It rode on his back as he pushed his bike to the entrance of the fairgrounds to wait for help to come.

Soon Tom arrived to find six sleepy, exhausted boys with large prizes and six bikes.

"I can see that you boys had a good time at the carnival," Tom said with a smile, remembering how it was when he was twelve years old at the carnival.

He loaded their bikes and asked everyone to jump in the back of his pick-up truck. He dropped each boy at his home, with his bike and prize.

For Rick and Joey, sleep was not far behind. The other boys were in dreamland as soon as their heads hit their pillows.

chapter six

THE KIDNAPPING

The next evening after supper, the boys met at the tree house to prepare for a new investigation.

When all the boys were gathered together, Mr. Spencer came outside to talk to the boys. "I want you boys home early. There is no sense in riding around in the dark. It could become a dangerous situation."

"No problem, Dad," Rick replied. "We will be home early. We have plans to ride over to the Meadowlands subdivision. If nothing happens, we'll be back soon."

"Okay," Dad said, "I just want you boys to be careful."

Then the boys mounted their bikes for their new investigation. The air was damp and the sun was sinking in the sky as Rick, Joey, Sam, Pete, Justin, Dillon and Garth pushed their bikes up the steep winding road to the top of the hill. The boys heard a car approaching quickly behind them. They steered their bikes as close to the side of the road as possible without hitting the guardrails that blocked the steep hill into the valley below. The automobile almost hit them as it sped past. It was a red and black sedan. They couldn't see who was driving, but they noticed only two men in the car.

"I can't believe that maniac who was driving that car!" Sam stuttered nervously. "Are you sure we should go over to Glenshaw? You know Glenshaw is where the gangs hang out. It's a really bad neighborhood. I'm afraid of what might happen."

"Yeah," Dillon spoke up. "Rick's dad told us to stay out of dangerous situations."

"Come on!" Justin called back to his friends. "We've gone this far, we might as well ride down the hill to the Meadowlands subdivision and see what's going on. Then we can decide if we want to go on or turn around at the Seventh Street Bridge and go back home."

"Okay, here's the plan," Rick said. "I agree with Justin. Let's ride over to the Meadowlands Subdivision first. I noticed several robberies marked there on the map that Dillon gave us. We can always ride to Glenshaw later if we don't find anything suspicious at Meadowlands."

As they were pedaling around the Meadowlands subdivision, they noticed all the lights on at 3417 County Street. Pete held out his hand to silently signal the boys to stop. "We'd better investigate that brick house over there," he whispered. "That's where Mr. and Mrs. Perkins live. My mom told me that Mrs. Perkins is in the hospital. I don't see Mr.

Perkins' car in the driveway. They never had all the lights on in the house at one time."

"Look," Garth said, pointing to the front window on the second floor. "Don't you see two boys in that bedroom? Do they have any teenagers?"

"I don't think so," Pete answered in a whisper. "They are both retired."

Rick spoke up. "Those two boys look just like the boys we helped to get arrested from the carnival. There were four of them and they were picking people's pockets. I was so glad that the Barker took action and called the police."

"Yeah," Justin replied. "They were acting so smart when the police hauled them away. I guess someone bailed them out of jail."

"I'll bet those boys are the ones who have doing the break-ins around here," Sam said.

"Maybe they're the ones who trashed the Wilson Elementary School!" Joey piped in.

"What'll we do if they're bigger than us?" Sam asked nervously. "I didn't pay any attention to how big they were when we saw them at the carnival. We don't want to get beaten up, do we?"

"No problem," Justin said. "If they try something stupid, I can get a good wrestling hold on one of them and you guys can overpower the rest of them."

"No, that would be stupid," Garth remarked. "We're on the side of the police, not on the side of gangs. We don't have to act mean and stupid like they do."

"Well," Rick said, "my dad always says there is safety in numbers. Also remember, we have our cell phones and if it gets too far out of hand, we can always call the police. Those boys don't know that we have cell phones with us."

The boys hid behind the hedges in the back yard of 3415 County Street. The F.B.I. Club members were close enough to hear what the teenagers were saying.

"Don't take anything more than you can carry," a mean voice told the other gang members. "We'll go right over to Sonny's Pawn Shop and unload our haul. We need the money. These people probably won't even miss their stuff." The gang put pillowcases of loot into the baskets on their bikes, which were hidden on the opposite side of the house.

"Let's stay hidden for a while," Garth suggested. "Rick, you can call the police now and give Chief Adams a report. That way they can have an undercover agent waiting for the gang to arrive at Sonny's. They'll be caught with the stolen loot. That should put a wrinkle in their robberies for a while."

"That's a great idea," Rick said. "I'll call the station and ask if Chief Adams is in. Maybe he will have an undercover agent who can come and catch the gang." Rick dialed the police station and told them what was about to happen. He hoped that the police would recover the stolen items right away. "These dudes are brazen!" Rick reported. "They act like they've robbed homes before. They don't think they'll get caught."

The officer on the other end of the line assured Rick that he would send an undercover officer to observe and record the transactions. Then a back-up squad would put them all under arrest. "Thanks for the tip, son. Here at the police station, we depend on tips to help in the capture of criminals," the officer told Rick.

The boys remained behind the hedges waiting for the thieves to leave. They congratulated themselves on a job well done by giving each other a silent high five.

Rick told the other boys, "We have to send a message to these gangs of robbers and thieves that we are not going to let them get away with crime in our city. Chief Adams will have his hands full when these thieves are brought into the police station."

"Yeah," Garth said, "we will help to reclaim our city. This will be a safer place to live now."

Justin, Sam, Pete, and Dillon agreed. They decided to ride away down the tree-lined road. Joey was the last to leave. The night was eerie. The streetlights gave a misty glow.

Suddenly the stillness was broken when Dillon called out, "Look at those dudes leaning against the cars over there! They look like mean gang members. Keep on pedaling so we can get out of here!"

"I told you we shouldn't come this way," Sam said, his voice trembling with fear. "Those dudes are probably the Red Bandana Gang, the worst gang in Glenshaw."

Loud noises and shouts rang out from across the street in front of the convenience store. The men were wearing red bandanas around their heads, blue jeans and red shirts with black printing on the front and back. They began to yell and whistle as the boys rode as fast as they could pedal past the convenience store. The streetlights made it easier to see the gang. They looked like they were asking for trouble.

"What are you kids doing riding down our street?" a tall gang member yelled to them. "What are you doing here? This is our side of town and we don't want any outsiders coming over here after dark." All the boys rode away as fast as their legs could pedal to escape the gang. With his shorter legs, Joey was still last in line.

Rick called back to Joey. "Hurry! Pedal as fast as you can. Hurry! They might hurt us."

The leader said to the gang, who were leaning on the red and black sedan in front of the convenience store, "I'll bet we could catch one of these kids and hold him for ransom." With a wave of his arm, the leader signaled to two men, one who was about 6'2" tall and 160 pounds. He was tall and skinny but had large bulging muscles. The other man was about 5'8" tall and weighed about 200 pounds. He was short and stocky and shouted out, "Who gave you kids permission to ride down our street?" Both men wore dirty, ragged clothes and looked like they hadn't combed their hair in months. They saw Joey, who was falling behind the other boys. The two men dashed across the street with their eyes on Joey.

One of them grabbed Joey, and the other picked up the bike and carried it back across the street to the waiting big red and black sedan with the engine running.

"Let me go!" Joey shouted, "I didn't do anything to you. We were just going for a joy ride."

"Then you can go for a joy ride with us. Shut up and be still before I hurt you," the big man said, as he covered Joey's eyes with a red bandana and laughed. The other members of the gang joined in with hideous laughter as they pushed Joey into the back seat of the waiting sedan.

"Holy Cow!" Rick shouted to the other boys. "Stop! Did you see those dudes take Joey and shove him into that red and black sedan? I knew I should have left him at home. What are we going to do?"

Just then, the red and black sedan passed the boys as they sped down the street.

"Did anybody get the license number?" Rick said, weeping.

"I didn't get it," Garth said. "That car sped by so fast it caught me by surprise."

In the meantime, Joey was pleading, "Please let me go!" He was very scared with his eyes blindfolded. He could hear the entire gang laughing. "I told you to shut up and be still or I'm gonna hurt you," the angry voice said. "You are our prisoner. No one rides down our street without our permission, especially at night."

"Boss," said one of the gang members, "let's take him to our hideout and call his parents and see if they'll pay us a tidy sum to get their precious brat back!"

"My friends will find me and you'll be sorry. Who are you anyway?" Joey asked, shivering because he was so "scarified." He thought they might kill him or do something worse than that.

The big man, who smelled and looked like he hadn't had a bath in a month, pushed Joey to the floor of the sedan. The odor of his body almost made Joey sick to his stomach.

"I don't want to hear another peep out of you. Do you understand?" the kidnapper threatened. "If your parents won't pay to get you back, then we have no other choice but to sell you to one of those slave traders who buy little boys like you. They'll pay a pretty price for a hard working boy of your age."

Joey replied tearfully, "My mom doesn't have any money, because she gets it from my dad. She has to ask my dad for money when she needs it. My dad is a detective, and he doesn't have any money either. I asked him for five dollars yesterday and he said he didn't have it. My mom and dad don't have any money." Then, Joey began to sob harder. He felt the car moving fast down the street and could feel every bump in the road. The boss man said, "No one will find him at our hideout," and then laughed hideously again. "We can contact the slave trader as soon as we get there." Joey began to cry and sob so hard his body shook all over.

"Shut up and be quiet! Don't you understand?" the big red bandana man said, as he pushed Joey back on the floor.

"Yes sir, I do," Joey responded, nervously as he continued to cry. His head was throbbing. He could feel his heart beating through his jacket. He was trying hard to think of what to do next. The thought of what Rick told him earlier filled his brain. "You are going to get into trouble, if you don't think first." So Joey sat there and thought about it. He thought about himself. He thought about his mom and dad and how sad they would be if he never went home again. He sure didn't want to get Rick into trouble either. "But what am I to do?" He had so many thoughts running around his brain, he was so confused. He remembered that his dad had told him to pray and God would answer his prayers. He tried to clear his brain. "How do I pray? Do I just ask God to get me out of this mess?" Then Joey bowed his head, folded his hands, and asked, "Dear God, if you're watching me right now, please tell me how to get out of this danger. Please don't let these maniacs kill me or sell me to the slave traders. I will try to listen to you for the answer. Love, Joey Spencer, the boy who was kidnapped."

Just then, he put his hand in his jacket pocket and felt the piece of paper with the cell phone numbers. "I'm in a real pickle, but I must try to find a way to escape," Joey mumbled to himself. He reached into his other jacket pocket and felt his mother's tiny cell phone. "Boy! I'm glad that I wrote the cell phone numbers of everyone. I'm glad that I was prepared this time," he thought to himself, as he carefully opened his mother's tiny cell phone. He felt the send button. He could dial 911. "What should I do?" Then he remembered Rick's cell phone number. "I know what to do! I'll call Rick and tell him I'm on the floor of this red and black sedan, blindfolded. And ask him to call the police to get help! Now, I have to push this blindfold up just a little bit off my eyes and scoot onto the back seat so I can see the street signs."

When the three men were talking to each other and not paying any attention to Joey, he pushed the blindfold up just enough to peek out of one eye. He dialed Rick's number. Nothing happened. He turned the phone off and on again, but the phone was dead. "What do I do now?" How could he tell Rick where he was and what was happening to him?" Then he heard a soft crackling sound under his jacket. "Yeah, I remember, Rick gave me a walkie-talkie. If I face the car door, I can talk into the walkie-talkie. These mean dudes can't hear me if I whisper. Maybe someone is listening. Is this the right thing to do?" he thought again to himself.

Joey slid back to the floor of the sedan and wiggled around on the floor until he was able to get the walkie-talkie from under his jacket. He pushed the Talk button and whispered nervously, "Rick, Rick, I'm kidnapped… red and black sedan."

Rick gave a sigh of relief when he heard Joey's whispers. "Hey guys," he said, "Joey is alive. I hope the police got the Amber Alert off fast. Those dudes looked dangerous."

Rick replied softly into the walkie-talkie, "Where are you, Joey? Are you okay? Give me your position."

Joey knelt on the floor of the sedan, and he was just tall enough to see out of the window with just a small opening in the blindfold. He pretended he was leaning on the window. "Raleigh Street, South Street, Columbia Street." He sat back on the floor of the sedan. He held the walkie-talkie close to his ear, so no one could hear that he was using it, and waited for an answer.

Rick understood the clues that Joey gave. He heard the noise of the running car engine in the background. After hearing the names of several streets, Rick knew the direction Joey was going. Suddenly Joey heard Rick's reply in a whisper. He pressed the receiver very close to his ear. Then he heard Rick's soft voice again. "We got your position, help is on the way."

Rick turned to the other boys and said frantically, "Joey's still kidnapped! He gave me some clues. It sounded like he was in a moving car. He said, 'red and black sedan.' He gave some more clues when he named the streets they were passing.

It sounds like they're heading for the pier at Water Street. We must get him help in a jiffy. I'm going to call 911 and ask if they got the Amber Alert started. We have to save Joey!"

Garth said, "Make sure you give them the clues Joey gave to you. With those clues, the police can find him quickly."

Joey inched his way up and sat on the back seat again. His heart was thumping so hard that he thought everyone in the car could hear it beating. Tears were still running down his face.

"Didn't I tell you to stay down on the floor?" the kidnapper said harshly, as he pushed Joey really hard to the floor of the car. He wanted to impress upon Joey just how serious he was. "If you get up again, I'm going to hurt you, boy. Now get down on the floor and stay there!!"

Soon police sirens came from behind to overtake the red and black sedan. The sedan squealed to a stop, almost hitting the police cruiser in front.

The police officer came out of the cruiser with his gun drawn. "Come out with your hands up," the officer ordered loudly.

The driver leaned his head out of the car window and asked sheepishly, "What do you want, officer? I didn't do anything wrong. I didn't break any traffic laws, did I?"

"Everyone out of the car with your hands up, that's what I want!" the officer ordered, pointing his gun towards the driver.

"But I didn't do anything wrong," the driver repeated. "What's your beef, officer? You ain't got any reason to stop me."

"Get out of the car now!" the officer demanded.

"All right!" the driver said, as he got out of the red and black sedan. "Do you have a search warrant?"

"I don't need one. Now, the rest of you get out of the car with your hands up and move over here," the officer ordered.

The big man, who smelled terrible, whispered to Joey, "Stay on the floor or I'm going to hurt you."

The officer went over to the car. He shined his flashlight into the car to check whether it was empty. He found Joey crouched on the floor, shaking with terror. The officer reached in, removed the blindfold and put his hand on Joey's shoulder. "Come on out of there, son. No one is going to hurt you. Go sit in my patrol car while I call for back-up." The officer pressed the mike that was clipped to his shoulder to call the station for assistance. Then he walked over to the kidnappers, who were being handcuffed by the officer's partner. "You guys are in a lot of trouble for kidnapping this child. I hope the judge throws the book at you."

As he finished his call for back-up, several patrol cars arrived with their lights flashing and sirens blasting. They frisked the men to be sure that they didn't have any weapons on them, and took them off to the police station.

The officer returned to the squad car and asked Joey, "Are you okay, Joey? You look like you had a very bad experience."

Still shaking all over, Joey answered, "I think I'm okay. They threatened to hurt me because I was crying."

The officer explained, "It's very important that you tell us everything they said to you. We will need those facts recorded when we get to the police station. Right now, let me take you to the police station. I'll call your parents. They will be very happy to know that you're alive and well. We put out the Amber Alert as soon as your friends called. You were very clever to call out the names of the streets and the color of the car. Otherwise, we would have had a harder time finding you."

When Joey and the officer arrived at the police station, Rick, Dillon, Justin, Sam, Pete and Garth had arrived, too. "I'm grateful to you boys," another officer said. "The Red Bandana Gang is responsible for other kidnappings and robberies. We just arrested the ringleader of The Red Bandana Gang. He was charged with kidnapping a little girl from the parking lot at the mall. Fortunately, that little girl remembered everything her parents and schoolteachers taught her about kidnappers. She was able to get away safe and sound. Thank goodness, she was not hurt. She was the bravest little girl I ever saw. She was even able to identify the license number of the getaway car."

Then Joey sat down with the Sergeant and answered all of his questions. He told the Sergeant the details about how he was kidnapped.

Within an hour, Joey was reunited with his parents. They both hugged him tightly and told him how much they loved him. "Now Joey, you are too young to be a Junior Investigator. You'll just have to wait until you're older and wiser," his mother said, with tears in her eyes. Finally, they took Joey home.

Later the next afternoon, Sam, Justin, Pete, Garth, and Dillon came over to the club house. They all met in the back yard. Joey came out of the house. He didn't look any different than when they had seen him at the police station the day before.

"You were so brave," Justin said, "but you still have to think of the consequences. You were not able to pedal as fast as the rest of us. That's why the kidnappers were able to capture you. You were in a lot of danger. We cannot be responsible for you all the time. You must wait until you're older to be a member. That's why Rick set the age at eleven-and-a-half years old."

"Okay," Joey said somberly. "I understand. Boy, it's hard growing up. I hope it gets easier from now on."

"Not to worry. Remember, you aren't a full F.B.I. Club member yet, but you're working on it," Dad said with a grin. Then he became more serious. "Remember, I warned you about the dangers. I was so worried when you did not come home early. Glenshaw is not a safe place for anyone except those who live there. You all violated their space."

"I'm so sorry, dad," Joey said soberly. "Is there anything I can do? I still want to help the Junior Investigators?"

"First of all, you must learn to follow orders. When Rick or I or your mother feel you are not ready to do something, you have to accept it graciously and wait until we know that you are ready."

"I know of something you can do for the junior investigators," Rick spoke up. "From now on, we will leave you at the club house. If we need help, we'll call you with instructions. But you will only become a real member when you're old enough. That is eleven-and-a-half years old."

"At least there's something I can do," Joey said excitedly. "I won't even need Mom's cell phone. I can use Dad's as soon as he gets home from work."

"Well, we certainly are getting experience in the investigation business," Sam said, laughing at how they had gotten on the wrong side of the Red Bandana Gang.

"We aren't done with investigating yet. We'll wait until tomorrow and go out again! This time we'll go to the neighborhoods we know. I don't want to put anybody in jeopardy again," Rick said to his friends.

"That's a good idea," Dillon said. "I was so scared when we rode to Glenshaw. I'm so glad that your brother kept his head and remembered everything we tried to tell him to do in case of an emergency. My mom is still talking about Joey's dangerous experience. She has called all of her friends to tell them of his kidnapping."

"My mom is calling all of her friends, too," Rick said. "She is so proud to know that my friends and I are good investigators and were able to help the police solve these crimes. If it weren't for Joey's fast thinking, he could have been seriously hurt. I can see that Joey is finally growing up to be a fine young man. I'm proud to call him my brother," Rick said, putting his arm around Joey's shoulder. "Come on, guys, let's go to the club house and plan our next investigation."

chapter seven

THE ROBBERS

Rick called everyone Friday night. He invited all of the junior investigators to come to a Sunday afternoon meeting at the F.B.I. Club house. Time passed quickly, and after church on Sunday, the boys were excited to get together again. Justin, Garth, Sam, Dillon and Pete arrived on time for the meeting. As the meeting was being called to order, Joey climbed up the ladder.

"Don't leave me out of the meeting," Joey said, almost out of breath. "Rick, why didn't you tell me you were having a meeting this afternoon? You know that I want to be a member of the F.B.I. Club too."

"You can't go out with us," Rick said. "You must stay here and handle any emergency from the club house. Don't you remember what you were told, when you were rescued from those kidnappers? Besides, Mom and Dad told both of us that you are not old enough to go out on our investigations."

"I remember what Mom and Dad said, but I still want to be a member of the F.B.I. Club, so I guess this will have to do for now," Joey replied sorrowfully.

"Are we going out to investigate a crime today?" Pete asked.

"Yes, we can check out the neighborhoods that Dillon's dad marked on the map," Garth added.

"Sure," Rick said. "I checked my notes from my research at the library. I compared them with the break-ins on the map. There were four house break-ins in the Westhaven subdivision. That's only a three-mile bike ride from here."

"I know that area," Garth agreed. "Several of my scouting friends live over there. They are really nice homes."

"Also, we might look in the areas surrounding the Tower Mall," Rick continued. "They've had three break-ins in the past three months. There were robberies at the Quick Mart, Farber's Clothes Shop, and Wilson's General Store. All the shops were robbed after they were closed. Each store lost a lot of merchandise."

"Let's do some surveillance at the businesses around the Tower Mall," Sam suggested. "That's only a couple of miles away."

"No, I think we need to go to Westhaven," Justin said. "Since this is the weekend, families will be going away for short vacations."

"Yeah, I second that," Pete chimed in. "I think we would have more luck catching crooks in Westhaven."

"Okay," was echoed by Sam, Garth, Dillon and Justin. "Let's go."

"Joey, you stay here and man the phone," Rick instructed. "If we get into trouble, we'll call you, and you can call the police. That will be your job."

"Okay, but I still want to be a member of the Junior Investigators," Joey said, hoping this job would get him into the club.

"One thing at a time, Joey. We'll talk to you about it when we get back," Rick said.

The boys climbed down the ladder, excited about the new adventure. They mounted their bikes and checked the batteries on their bike and helmet headlights. The sky was cloudy. The air was calm as they rode their bikes toward Westhaven.

"Maybe the sun will come peaking out from behind the clouds," Dillon said as he scanned the horizon, hoping the day would prove fruitful. Maybe they could solve another crime.

"Have you checked your cell phones?" Rick asked.

"Yes," Garth said, "I took mine off the charger when I left home."

"Mine has enough charge," Pete said. "It was charged this morning and I haven't used it very much today."

"My batteries are half-charged," Dillon said, "I have enough battery for tonight, but I'll put it on the charger when I go home anyway."

"I'm sorry, Rick," Sam said. "My battery is lower than I thought. I am going to shut it off. I'll turn it on if I have to use it. That will save the battery."

"That's all right, Sam," Rick replied. "We have enough cell phones here that you won't need to worry."

"My mom just bought me a new cell phone," Justin said. "She said it had free minutes after nine o'clock in the evening and free calls Saturday and Sunday. I took it off the charger when I left home. Since we all seem to be ready, let's go!"

"I agree!" Sam echoed. "Let's ride out to see if we can solve a crime today. Then hopefully we will all come home safe and sound. We want to help the police catch gangsters, robbers and thieves. We are making our neighborhood a good place to live. The criminals know we are patrolling here, and crime is going down."

The boys headed down Columbia Street, crossing over the Seventh Street Bridge on their way to Westhaven.

Rick put his right hand up to signal everyone to come to a halt. "This is the Westhaven area," Rick explained, checking his map. "Here is Columbia Street and here we are." He pointed to the map. "Let's ride down to Dartmouth Street. That's where the last break-in happened. Let's all keep our eyes open."

As they made a left turn onto Dartmouth Street, Sam was paying very close attention to the fourth house on the right.

He could see people moving around outside, but was too far away to see who they were.

"There are Wendy, Sarah and Jennifer Thompson," Sam said, as they rode close enough to see them better. "It looks like they've been to the beach. Hi, girls!" Sam waved as they rode over to talk to them.

"Did you girls go to the beach today?" Garth asked.

"Hi, Garth," Sarah said. "No, we're just getting back from the city pool."

"Hi, Sam," Jennifer said, smiling. "We missed you at the pool. Aren't you working as a lifeguard at the pool anymore?"

"Not this week," Sam replied. "There were seven of us who qualified and finished the lifeguard training. We each alternate every two weeks working at the pool. I'll be working again next week."

"Hi, Wendy," Dillon remarked. "We missed you at Sunday School last week. Are you planning to go next Sunday?"

"Yes, I am," Wendy replied. "I was visiting my grandmother last weekend. What brings you guys to our neighborhood?"

"We've been doing Citizen Patrol in your neighborhood," Rick spoke up, "and we're helping the police catch the crooks."

"Yeah," Garth said. "We've done such a good job that we haven't had any break-ins for several weeks. The crooks are scared to come into our neighborhood. They know if we see them, we'll call the police."

"That makes me feel better," Jennifer said. "Mom won't let us play outside after it gets dark. I hope you can do the same for our neighborhood, and chase the crooks and robbers away."

"We're going to try our best," Pete said. "It was nice to see you girls again, but we need to get back to our patrolling now."

The boys waved good-bye as they rode farther down Dartmouth Street. All the boys were looking at each house and checking to be sure that nothing strange was going on.

As they approached the end of Dartmouth, Mr. Douglas saw them riding their bikes toward his house.

"Hi, boys," Mr. Douglas called as he was cutting his hedges.

"Hi, Mr. Douglas," Pete said, as he waved to Mr. Douglas.

The boys rode up his driveway to where he was working.

"Hi, everyone," Mr. Douglas said. "What are you boys doing over here in our neighborhood?"

"We're the F.B.I. Club, the Famous Boy Investigators Club. We are on patrol in your area looking for break-ins," Pete spoke up, and the boys asked Mr. Douglas about crimes in his neighborhood.

"Have you seen any strangers driving or walking around here recently?" Rick asked. "I did some research about break-ins here in Westhaven. Also, I have compared them to our map."

"Could I see the map?" Mr. Douglas asked, as he put his hedge clippers in his wheelbarrow. He took the map from Rick and examined it carefully. "My wife and I were the first to build out here. I know everyone who has moved into Westhaven. I've heard about the break-ins. I've been keeping my eyes open when I'm not at work. I feel so much better knowing a group of young investigators are on patrol. That should tell the crooks, thieves, and robbers to stay out of our neighborhood."

"I'm glad that you have confidence in our group," Rick said. "We've done such a good job in our neighborhood that there hasn't been a break-in for several weeks."

"It was good to see you again, Mr. Douglas," Pete said, "but, we need to get back to our patrolling."

"God bless you boys, and stay safe," Mr. Douglas said, as he waved good-bye to his young friends.

The boys rode their bikes out of Mr. Douglas's driveway and continued down to the end of Dartmouth Street, where they waved to Garth's friend, Tom Williams.

They turned right onto Mt. Vernon Avenue and then rode down Park Avenue. The streets in Westhaven appeared to be quiet. They saw children of all ages playing in front yards, older people sitting on swings on front porches, and boys washing cars in front of their garages.

"We've been riding for several hours and everything seems to be quiet here. So let's ride down Main Street towards Oakdale," Sam said. "If everything stays quiet, we can always get a burger and an ice cream sundae at Dairy Queen."

"Sounds like a good idea to me," Justin said. "All this pedaling is making me hungry!"

"Yes," Garth agreed, "and it's getting late. It's almost six o'clock and I'm getting hungry, too."

Rick, Pete, Sam, and Dillon all agreed. The boys headed out of the Westhaven subdivision and rode back to the Seventh Street Bridge toward Oakdale. Then they turned left onto Main Street, heading for the Dairy Queen. It was approaching seven o'clock in the evening.

They noticed cars parked along the curb. Most of the stores had closed for the day, and only their storefront security lights remained on. At first glance, the boys noticed something strange: there were no lights at all in the hardware store, which everyone knew closed at 5:30 on Saturdays and Sundays.

There was an eerie feeling about the street. Something just didn't look right. The sun was going down and the air was calm.

"Rick," Dillon called out, "look up there at Sullivan's Hardware Store. All of its lights are off. They close at 5:30 on Sundays. Something doesn't feel right to me."

"I agree," Rick responded. "I think we'd better investigate."

The five young investigators continued down Main Street, getting closer to the hardware store. They rode up and stopped in front of the store. All of a sudden, loud banging sounds came from the back of the hardware store. The boys kept totally quiet and knelt down in front of the display window to get a better look. They listened intently to the sounds. Bang! Crash!! Bang! Crash! The muffled banging continued at a steady pace.

"What could that be, Rick?" Dillon asked. "It sounds like it's coming from the back of the building."

"I don't know, but we'd better investigate," Rick said with apprehension. "It sounds like they're trying to destroy the store."

"Let's park our bikes in front of the Dollar Store next door. That way, it will look like they're for sale," Garth said, hoping they could make a quick getaway if trouble began to brew.

Justin suggested, "Let's creep around the corner and go down the alley between the drug store and the hardware store. Then we'll be able to see what's going on."

"Sam, you go first," Rick offered. "I have my cell phone ready to dial the police if it's a robbery or vandals or something like that."

"Okay, if you want, I'll go first," Sam replied. "Give me the night vision binoculars. I think I can identify the situation better with them."

"Here you go," Rick replied, as he took the binoculars from around his neck and passed them to Sam.

Sam held his breath as he peered around the corner of the building. He saw four men wearing black jogging pants and black jackets. They were carrying boxes of merchandise and throwing them into the back of an eighteen-wheeler truck.

"This is a real robbery in progress," Sam said, as he brought his head around and whispered to Rick, "You'd better call 911 now! I think this is the Black Hooded Gang from across the river. There are four of them that I can see. I don't know if there are any more gang members inside the store. They might even have guns! I'm scared."

"Yeah! I read about them in the local newspaper when I did my research at the library," Rick whispered to Sam. "We need more unmarked police cars patrolling the streets at night."

Rick crept to the Dollar Store, where he dialed 911. When Rick heard the dispatcher answer the phone, he whispered, "There's a robbery in progress at 304 Main Street. We are down the alley beside the drug store. Sullivan's Hardware Store is being robbed. You'd better send the police right away before they clean out the store," he said nervously.

"Son, how many robbers do you see?" the dispatcher asked.

"There are four of them, wearing all black clothes, that I can see," Rick answered, "but there could be more."

"We're sending a unit now," the dispatcher told him. "What are the culprits doing?"

"They're in the back of the building loading a large box truck," Rick responded.

"Son, you stay where you are and be very quiet," the dispatcher instructed. "The police should be there in the next few minutes."

In less than five minutes, Justin saw three police cars coming down Main Street.

"I'll be right back, Justin," Rick said, "I'm going to show the police where the thieves are. I can still hear the gang loading the truck. The robbers don't know that we're watching them."

Rick called Joey to report in. "Have you found any crimes yet?" Joey asked.

"Yes," Rick told Joey, "Sullivan's Hardware store is being robbed and we have it under surveillance. The police are on their way. Stay at the clubhouse. I'll call you if we need anything. I'll tell you all about it when we get home."

"Right! Roger! Okay!" Joey replied. "I'll do anything I can to help you. Do you want me to call Dad and put him on alert?"

"I don't think so right now. I just called 911," Rick replied.

Rick crept back down along the wall of the drug store toward Main Street. He stood at the curb as the police were getting closer. Chief Adams was in the first car. He stopped at the curb next to Rick and opened his window.

Rick motioned to Police Chief Adams. He handed the night vision binoculars through the open window of the patrol car. The chief noticed that Rick was pointing toward the robbery in progress. The Chief saw that Sam, Garth, Pete, and Dillon were crouched down safely down in front of the display window of the hardware store.

Then the Chief closed the window of his patrol car and said, in a calm but authoritative voice, "C-14, C-14, proceed around the block toward the back of Sullivan's Hardware Store. Hold your position until I give the signal. N-20, N-20, proceed to the corner of Main and Pine streets. Set up a roadblock and keep any traffic from coming down either street. We have a dangerous situation on our hands."

The radio crackled after he lifted his finger from the mike.

Police Chief Adams got out of his patrol car and peeped around the corner of the drug store. Using the night vision binoculars, he recognized two men from the F.B.I.'s Ten Most Wanted poster. He stepped back, turned, and called the police dispatcher. "Call the F.B.I. and inform them that we are about to arrest two of the F.B.I.'s Most Wanted fugitives. I'll keep you informed of the ongoing events. The junior investigators who reported this crime are safe, secure, and out of sight." The Chief crept over to where the boys were hiding below the hardware store window. Chief Adams approached the boys and whispered, "This could become a very dangerous situation, and I don't want any of you boys to get hurt, so go over to Sam's Grocery Center across the street and stay out of sight. I will be over to see you when this situation is under control. Right now it's my duty to wait for the F.B.I. officers to arrive."

In a few minutes, the F.B.I. agents arrived on the scene. They met Chief Adams at the curb. The F.B.I. agents Patterson and Lewis flashed their badges to Chief Adams and said, "We are Federal Agents and we were instructed to come to this address. Where are the fugitives?"

"They're down the alley behind the hardware store. There are several other robbers down there, too. I haven't found out just how many there are." Chief Adams motioned to the F.B.I. agents to follow him to the corner, where they could safely view the robbery in progress.

"Here, use these night vision binoculars and look around the corner at the truck," Chief Adams instructed.

Bang! Crash! Bang! Crash! Everyone could hear the men rapidly loading the back of the truck with the stolen merchandise.

"We'd better block off the alley and bring this case to a close, as quickly as we can," F.B.I. agent Lewis said.

"I have two patrol cars in place and ready to move in," Chief Adams informed the F.B.I. agents. "I'll give the signal."

"I want to be sure that this is my collar," Police Chief Adams said to Agents Patterson and Lewis.

"That will not be a problem," Agent Patterson assured the Chief. "We just want to take custody of the two fugitives after you book and process all the robbers."

"C-14, C-14, N-20, N-20," Chief Adams said into the mike he had clipped to his shoulder, "we're ready to move in. Keep your eyes open and don't let anyone get away."

Chief Adams and Agent Patterson rounded the back of the drug store with their guns drawn. "Stop where you are!" Chief Adams ordered. "Get off that truck with your hands up! No funny business!"

Two men, wearing all black clothes, looked at each other with surprise. They both looked in different directions, to see where they could run.

"Get your hands up like I said!" Chief Adams' voice got louder. "You're under arrest!"

Suddenly, the two men jumped off the back of the truck. One man took off running on the far side of the truck from where Chief Adams and Agent Patterson were approaching.

"I'll get this one," Agent Lewis yelled, as he took off running after the fugitive. In about five hundred feet, Agent Lewis tackled the escapee. "You're under arrest," Agent Lewis said with a satisfied snicker, as he pulled his handcuffs out, grabbed the man's left arm, slapped the cuffs to his wrist, pulled his right arm around his back, and with a jerk attached the cuff to his right wrist.

The gang member lay on the ground, completely dazed. "Get up!" Agent Lewis instructed. "You're under arrest for burglary, resisting arrest, and receiving stolen goods. We've been looking for you and your brother for a year and a half." Agent Lewis escorted the suspect back to the truck.

Chief Adams already had his suspect handcuffed and had read him his Miranda Rights. Agent Patterson pushed another suspect against the side of the truck. "Spread your legs and step back," Agent Patterson said sternly, as he frisked one of the fugitives. "He has a gun!" Agent Patterson alerted the officers, as he pulled the gun out of the man's back pocket. "Man, you are just racking up the charges. You're looking at a five-year mandatory sentence for carrying a weapon during a robbery."

The three suspects were handcuffed to the tailgate of the truck. Agent Lewis stood guard over the prisoners. Chief Adams and Agent Patterson entered the back of the hardware store with their guns drawn and demanded, "This is the F.B.I.! If there's anybody in here, you'd better come out now with your hands up in the air."

One man came out from the storeroom. He looked like he was reaching for a gun.

"If you move a muscle, mister, I'll drop you where you stand. Now, drop that gun and put your hands up like I told you in the first place," Police Chief Adams said with authority. "I don't want to shoot anybody today. Drop your gun!"

The man, dressed in black, paused and, seeing himself out-numbered, dropped the weapon. He reluctantly raised his hands.

"Now, that's better," Police Chief Adams said, as he handcuffed the criminal. "We don't allow robbers in this town. Can you explain why you were robbing this store?"

"It's none of your business what we were doing. Our boss sent us. Besides, you have to prove that we're robbing this store," the ringleader said, sneering.

"Okay, you can tell it to the judge. He can sort out the gory details. Right now, you're under arrest for suspicion of robbery, carrying a concealed weapon, possession of stolen goods and resisting arrest," Chief Adams said. Then he cleared his throat and read all of the prisoners their Miranda Rights word for word, so there wouldn't be any problems later.

Agent Patterson, Chief Adams, and the three crooks made their way back to the front of the hardware store, where Chief Adams' patrol car was parked. The two other police cars arrived with a gang member in the back seat of each patrol car. Chief Adams put one of the robbers in the back of his patrol car, and the two fugitives that the F.B.I. was looking for were placed in the back of Agent Lewis's patrol car. Now that all the criminals were in custody, Chief Adams walked across the street to Sam's Grocery Center to talk to Rick and his friends.

"Congratulations on your excellent surveillance, boys, but I must also warn you that you must be careful and stay out of sight. I'll have another patrol car here soon to secure the crime scene. I appreciate your surveillance, but you must remember that this is police work. It's our job to hunt for clues, apprehend criminals, and take them off to jail. You must be careful that the crooks don't hurt you like they did to Mrs. Bennett and your brother, Joey," Chief Adams lectured.

After the robbers were hauled off to jail, another F.B.I. agent pulled up and asked, "Do you need any further assistance?"

"No, the situation is under control," Chief Adams said. "Agent Lewis has the two fugitives in custody. I sent one of my men to accompany the fugitives and agent Lewis. Soon they'll be on the way to the federal lock-up, thanks to these young boys who did the surveillance work and called to let us know that the hardware store was being robbed. The gang cut the wires to the security system. They thought they could steal the entire contents of the hardware store before it opened on Monday morning."

When all the excitement was over and the robbers hauled off to jail, F.B.I. Agent Patterson crossed the street to congratulate the boys for a job well done.

"Officer Patterson, I'm so glad you came over," Chief Adams said. "I want you to meet these famous young men. They are the members of the F.B.I. Club here in town and have done a great service to Mayfield. In fact, if a crime is being committed around town, the criminals should be on their toes because the F.B.I. Club members are on the prowl."

"What does F.B.I. stand for?" Officer Patterson asked.

"The Famous Boy Investigators Club," Rick said proudly. "We are always on patrol looking for crimes taking place. Then we call the police so they can catch and arrest the gang members, robbers, and thieves."

"It makes me feel good to meet young men like you who have a burning desire to become F.B.I. Agents. I suggest you look into the requirements that you will need in High School to go into law enforcement," F.B.I. agent Patterson said to Rick, Sam, Justin, Dillon, Pete, and Garth.

"We will keep that in mind," Rick responded. "I want to be a detective just like my dad. I was amazed at how quickly Police Chief Adams recognized the two fugitives."

"Easy," Agent Patterson replied. "It's just good old police work."

"We'd better go now," Pete said. "We never made it to the Dairy Queen and I'm still hungry. What do you guys think?"

Chief Adams interrupted and said, "Hold up, boys, it's too dark now for you to ride your bikes down Main Street. I've called your parents. They all are on their way to take you and your bikes home. Maybe they'll take you to Dairy Queen for a celebration."

"I want a hot dog and milk shake," Garth said. "All this work has made me hungry, too."

The boys waited patiently with Chief Adams in the safety of the patrol car. Soon Garth's dad drove down Main Street, stopped at the curb, got out of his pick-up truck, and hugged Garth warmly. "I'm glad you're all right and that the criminals have been captured. Let me put your bike in the back of the truck. Do any of you boys need a ride?" Garth's dad asked.

"No, but we all want to go to Dairy Queen for our supper. Will you and Garth go with us?" Rick asked.

"You bet!" Garth's dad replied.

Pete's brother, Tom, who was searching for the boys, saw the police car and pulled over. Seeing Pete, Tom shouted, "Hey, Pete, are you all right, buddy?"

"Sure, I'm okay. It was so exciting! I even met a real F.B.I. agent. He was awesome. Would you ask Chief Adams if you could take me to Dairy Queen? Are Mom and Dad coming too?"

"No, they sent me because I have the truck. It can carry all the bikes. Can I use your cell phone so I can let Mom and Dad know that you are safe and not hurt? I don't want them to worry any more."

"Good idea," Pete answered. "I don't want them to worry either. We were on our way to Dairy Queen when we heard the Bang! Crash! Bang! The noise was coming from the hardware store. It was getting rather late, but we are junior investigators and we had to investigate the noise. That's when we found a robbery in progress."

Soon, Detective Spencer pulled up looking for Rick. "Are you okay, son? You had me worried when I got the call from the police dispatcher. I'm so glad you're safe."

"I'm okay, Dad," Rick said. "Did you bring Joey with you?" Dad and Rick gave each other a fond embrace. Rick continued, "We followed the rules and kept out of sight. We did our surveillance and as soon as we knew a robbery was in progress, we called the police. Chief Adams recognized two of the F.B.I.'s Most Wanted Fugitives, and he alerted the F.B.I. They came quickly and assisted Chief Adams to take charge of the situation. We had left our last surveillance at Westhaven subdivision and were heading for Dairy Queen. That's when all of this happened. We are still hungry and want to go to D.Q. Will you take me there?"

"No, I didn't bring Joey with me. When I got the call, I rushed down here. We can get him something and take it home with us."

In a few minutes, Sam's dad arrived in his work truck. He got out and gave Sam a big bear hug. "Are you okay, son? I was frightened when I got the call from the police. I'm so happy to see that you're safe. This investigative business is scary for the parents as well as for you boys," Sam's dad said.

"Everything is okay, Dad," Sam said, with a tear in his eye. "We had a fantastic adventure! I even spoke to the F.B.I.

agent. He was so brave, he even asked us to think about becoming F.B.I. agents when we grow up."

"Wow, Sam," his dad replied in amazement, "you did have quite an experience. This is one investigation you will never forget."

"Will you take me to Dairy Queen?" Sam urged. "The other boys and their parents are going there to celebrate with the F.B.I. Club."

In a few minutes, a green pick-up truck came down the street and pulled over to the curb. Dillon's dad got out of the truck and grabbed his son. He gave him a big bear hug. "I'm so glad that you're safe and sound. The policeman who called me only gave me a few details. You can fill me and your mother in later."

"Dad," Dillon asked. "Will you take me to D.Q.? The other parents are going, too. I'm hungry and with all this investigative work, I need some food. Like a milkshake and a hamburger."

"Sure thing, son," Mr. Notz said. "Put your bike in the back and we'll go to D.Q."

Finally, a dark blue pick-up truck arrived on the scene. Justin's dad hopped out of the truck and began to search through the crowd for his son. Justin saw his dad first, and ran to his open arms.

"Gee Dad," Justin said. "I'm so glad you're here at last. What took you so long?"

Justin's dad looked shocked as he replied, "Your mother and I have been so nervous wondering what had happened to you, because we thought you were only going for daylight surveillance today. You mother was so upset when the police called us that she stayed at home. She's waiting to hear your voice. You should be the one to give her the good news."

"Sure thing, dad," Justin replied. "I have the cell phone here and I'll call her right away."

All the parents agreed to take the junior investigators to Dairy Queen, where all the boys ordered their food. The boys ate hungrily while talking about the capture of the Black Hooded Gang. There was lots of laughing and excitement to go around. After they finished their food, each boy joined his parents for a ride to the club house.

On the way, Garth said that he wanted to call his mother. "I want to share the excitement of the day with her," Garth beamed. "She will be so proud that we are catching crooks and making our neighborhood safe for everyone." Garth then dialed his home number and spoke to his mother. They chatted a long time.

On their way home, the boys smiled as they passed Sullivan's Hardware Store. They all had the great satisfaction of knowing just how important their neighborhood watch was to their community.

The parents dropped the boys off at Rick's house to spend the night at the club house. They parked their bikes at the base of the old oak tree. Joey stuck his head out of the clubhouse window and demanded, "Tell me what happened! Who was breaking into the hardware store?"

The boys quickly climbed the ladder to the club house.

"Hold on Joey," Justin said. "We've got so much to tell you."

The boys took turns telling Joey about the excitement of the evening. They slid into their sleeping bags, fell asleep talking and began dreaming of gangs, robbers, and crooks.

Sam kept repeating in his sleep, "This business is harder than it looks." He was reliving his last investigation.

The boys awoke at the crack of dawn, ready for a man-sized breakfast. They discussed their investigations with Rick's dad and were eager to begin a new investigation soon. Then they hopped on their bikes and headed for their homes.

chapter eight

THE REWARD

The next morning, Rick and Joey went through the newspaper looking for the police report about the robbery at Sullivan's Hardware Store. Rick was so proud of how the F.B.I. Club members had worked together to help the police. Their detective work had really paid off. Rick said to his dad, "Our neighborhood should be a quieter, safer place now that those robbers are in jail."

Dad agreed. "I certainly hope so, Rick."

Joey interrupted, "Where is the article about the robbery and capture of those bad men?"

Dad said, "I have the article right here. It mentions the F.B.I. Club's quick thinking and how you assisted the police. Now others will know of your good deeds. Someday you may become a famous police detective."

The phone rang, and Mr. Spencer answered, "Hello. Yes, Chief, Rick is right here. Son, this is Chief Adams and he wants to speak to you."

The chief explained to Rick how proud he was of the F.B.I. Club. He had spoken to the mayor and the town councilmen, and they planned to give an award to Rick and the other investigators! "A ceremony will be held at the council meeting next week. In a few days, each family will be receiving an invitation in the mail to attend the awards ceremony. The mayor will give each boy a letter of commendation." The Chief said he was giving Rick the honor of telling the club members about the award first. Then he ended his phone call by repeating how proud he was of the Junior Investigators and their dedication to the community. Before hanging up, Rick thanked the Chief for his support of the Junior Investigators, and explained that it took all six boys working hard together to help catch those robbers.

That afternoon, Rick called a special meeting of the F.B.I. Club. When the boys were all assembled, Rick made his special announcement. "Chief Adams called me today and asked me to tell you some terrific news. He wants to give each of us a special commendation for our bravery. We are to attend the town council meeting next Tuesday evening at seven o'clock. Don't forget to invite your parents and friends. You will receive a special invitation by mail. There will probably be a photographer from the newspaper at the meeting. Is that all right with everyone's schedule?"

Each boy answered. "Yes, I can make it," Sam replied.

"Count me in," Pete said. "My mom will be so proud of me because I'm not a couch potato any more."

"Sure thing," Dillon added, "I'll be there. I hope my mom and dad come. I guess they'll have to bring my little sister, too."

Justin said, "Yes for me too."

Garth said, smiling, "Can I invite my scoutmaster, Mr. Byrum?"

"Yes, good idea," Rick replied. "Chief Adams said we could invite anyone we wished. That way your scout troop will get some publicity too."

"Do you think we might get our picture in the newspapers?" Garth asked.

"I think so. The chief told me there will be a press conference and some newspaper reporters, too. I hope we get a lot of publicity about our club," Rick stated. "Maybe we can help get some other clubs started."

"Wow!" Joey shouted. "Can you believe it? We're going to be famous!"

"That's not why we're getting the commendations," Rick replied. "We learned good detective skills. Also, we followed the rules by calling the police before the situation got out of hand. Now, let's get organized for the award ceremony. I think we had better meet at the Council Chambers at 100 Main Street at six-thirty. That will give us plenty of time to get a good seat up front."

"Yes, I agree," Dillon replied. "My mom, dad and I will be there on time. We might even have to bring my little sister. I hope she doesn't make a fuss."

"I'm so proud to be a member of the F.B.I. Club," Garth said. "But I really didn't expect to become famous already!" he added, as he and the other guys mounted their bikes to head home.

On Tuesday evening, Rick, Joey, Sam, Pete, Garth, Dillon, and Justin arrived at the town hall at six-thirty with their parents and Dillon's little sister.

Chief Adams ushered the boys into his office for a greeting and to prepare them for the reporters. "I'm so proud to meet and know all of you young men," Chief Adams said. "It seems that we only hear about how much crime is out there, and not enough on how good young people can be."

"Chief Adams," Rick said, "I want to thank you on behalf of our Junior Investigators for asking us to come here and receive this award. I was hoping that we could get some publicity about our F.B.I. Club when we meet the reporters from the newspapers and the TV station, WZAX. This is greater than I ever could have imagined."

"I'm glad you boys could be here," Chief Adams said. Then he drew Rick aside and lowered his voice. "Rick, I spoke to your dad yesterday and he told me that you didn't want Joey to become a member of the F.B.I. Club. First, you have to remember that Joey helped in each of the investigations and that he will be eleven-and-a-half in just six months. Now would be the right time for you to give him membership. It would be a great gesture on your part."

"Let me think about it," Rick said. "I'd have to call a special meeting to get a vote from the other members."

"That would be fine," Chief Adams said. "Joey and I will step out for a few minutes and you can call us when you're finished."

Rick called the other boys over and explained the situation. He called the special meeting to order and asked for a vote on Joey becoming a member. "We don't have time for a discussion, so just say yea or nay."

In a few minutes, Rick came out of the chief's office. "We had our meeting," Rick said. "I will make the announcement later in the ceremony, if you don't mind."

"This ceremony really is for you and your investigators, so I think it will be just fine," the chief said. Then he grinned. "Rick, I know your dad very well. He will be so proud of you and your investigators. He is a very intelligent man. I was so impressed with his work that I sent him to the Police Academy to learn about being a detective. I then had him transferred from walking the beat to the crime division, and he learned more. Education seems to go on for the rest of our lives."

"I plan to go to the Police Academy too," Rick bragged to the chief, "as soon as I graduate high school. I want to be the best detective this city has ever known. I want to be as good a detective as my dad."

"That's a very good goal for you to strive for," Chief Adams said, smiling. "Keep your grades up and your eyes on your goal. I know that you will be every bit as good as your father. In fact, you might even be good enough to take over my job when I retire."

"Did you know that my dad is a fireman?" Sam spoke up. "He is also a safety inspector. He inspected the tree house that we built for all the safety requirements and said we did a wonderful job."

Pete interrupted, "He gave us an official certificate that our tree house met all the safety and construction requirements. I hung the certificate on the front door of the club house."

"That was a great accomplishment for any young boys of your size," Chief Adams replied. "Now, it's time to get ready. You'll be surprised at the amount of publicity you will receive from the reporters," he explained. "There will be three newspaper reporters and someone from the TV station, WZAX. So with that in mind, let me escort you boys into the Town Hall meeting room to the waiting reporters. Relax, be yourselves, and know that I'll be here with you all the way through the interview."

As Chief Adams opened the door, the boys observed a large crowd inside. Cameras flashed around the room. Microphones on poles were pointed toward the boys. The reporters were whispering to each other. Several reporters started asking questions at the same time. "How did you solve those crimes? Are you going to testify against the culprits in court? Do you think you are heroes?" The questions came so fast and furiously that the boys didn't know what to say.

Police Chief Adams stepped forward and told the reporters, "Please ask one question at a time. It is not fair for you to bombard these young men with so many questions at once. To answer one of your questions, yes, these boys are heroes. They have shown that they care about their city. I would like to introduce the spokesman for the F.B.I. Club, Rick Spencer."

The crowd began to applaud and cheer. Rick stepped up to the microphone and stood next to the chief.

"How long have you boys been investigating?" Betty McNiven, reporter for The Daily Southerner, asked.

"This is our first year," Rick stated. "We did learn the rules and we only conducted surveillance. When we were sure a crime was being committed, we called the police to take over and arrest the criminals."

"What is the F.B.I. Club?" Betty McNiven asked.

"It stands for the Famous Boy Investigators," Rick responded.

"What does the Famous part mean?" Ms. McNiven continued.

"Ma'am," Rick replied, "I have carefully chosen a group of boys who want to be famous and reach their goals in life.

My goal is to be a famous detective, because I enjoy research and following through with clues. Together we learned how to look for clues. Why don't you ask each of the other boys what their goals are? I think you will be surprised to learn that everyone has their own special goal."

Chief Adams leaned down to Rick. "Why don't you introduce the other Junior Investigators to the reporters," he suggested.

"Sure thing, Chief," Rick replied proudly, as he pointed to Pete. "This is Pete Martinez. He is new to Mayfield. Next to him is my brother, Joey. Then, Sam Davis, who is vice president of our club, and over there is Garth Waters. He is a Boy Scout and is active in the community. Next to the last is Justin Stewart. He is a state wrestling champion. The one on the end is Dillon Notz. He works with his dad mowing lawns."

Wanda Fish stood up. "Hi, I'm Wanda Fish from the Mayfield Times; my question is directed to Pete Martinez. Since you are new to Mayfield, where did you move from?"

"I moved here with my parents and my grandmother from Puerto Rico," Pete replied. "My dad is an engineer. My grandmother is not well, so my mom stays home and takes care of her."

"How old are you, Pete?" Wanda Fish continued, "and do you enjoy being a Junior Investigator?"

"I'm eleven-and-a-half," Pete answered, "and yes, I enjoy the investigations. One time, we spotted a broken window. We found a woman who had been robbed and was tied up with ropes. We came to her rescue. Rick called for the ambulance and the police. I think we saved that woman's life. We not only save lives but we also do surveillance and search for clues."

"That was very brave of you boys to enter a house that had been robbed, because the robbers could have been hiding there and could have hurt you," reporter Wanda Fish exclaimed.

Pete explained, "You're right, but we heard a moaning sound. We knew someone was hurt, so we took the risk."

"What do you want to be when you grow up, Pete?" Wanda Fish asked.

"I want to be a famous computer programmer. I would rather use my mind than my muscles," Pete stated very seriously.

"That's a great career to explore. We're now in the time of cyberspace exploration, and the sky is the limit," reporter Wanda Fish reminded everyone. "Don't forget that your brain is a muscle that needs a lot of exercise, too." The audience laughed aloud at her comment.

"I didn't think about it that way, but I guess you're right," Pete said, smiling.

Betty McNiven from the Daily Southerner spoke up again. "What do you boys do for fun?"

"Well, we helped put up the booths and the prizes at the carnival last week," Dillon answered. "We also did odd jobs and gathered aluminum cans to raise money to build a tree house for our club. It's in Rick's back yard. We did have a little adult help. Still, we all worked hard and had fun, too."

"Hi, I'm Joe House, from the Mayfield News," another reporter broke in. "This question is directed to Rick. I see Joey is quite young. What are the age requirements for your club?"

"Joey is my brother. He's not quite a member of the F.B.I. Club yet, but he is working toward it," Rick said. "He has to be eleven-and-a-half in order to become a full member."

Joey stood up from his chair. He was sure that everyone could hear his knees knocking. "My name is Joey Spencer and I just turned eleven. My brother Rick won't let me join yet, but the tree house is in our back yard, so part of the tree house belongs to me too."

The reporters laughed and so did the parents. Then Joe House, the star reporter from the Mayfield News, continued with the interview. "How did you earn the money to build your tree house?"

"We gathered aluminum cans and took them to the Recycling Center. Also, we did odd jobs. After we put our money together, we had five hundred five dollars and thirty-five cents," Joey said. "Pete's brother Tom drove us and the cans to the Recycling Center. It cost us exactly five hundred dollars to build the tree house."

"Now I understand why you are called the Famous Boy Investigators," Joe House said. "You have used many skills to accomplish a very challenging task for boys your age. I wish that other young people would follow your example and try to do something constructive for their city. If everyone else was doing what you're doing with crime watch, it would greatly reduce the crime rate."

Ms. Betty McNiven asked, "Joey, what is your goal?"

"Even though I'm not a full member yet, I crawled on my hands and knees to get the license number off the River Rat Gang's van. It was because of our investigations that they were caught and put in jail."

"Do you want to be a detective when you grow up?" Betty McNiven asked.

"No way!" Joey answered, "I want to be a body builder. I exercise every day with my two-pound dumbbells. See my muscles? Charles Atlas is my idol. If he could be the strongest man in the world, then I think I can be, too."

"Being the strongest man in the world would be an excellent accomplishment. Remember, it is just as important to eat your fresh fruits and vegetables as it is to exercise," Betty McNiven replied. "Ask your dad about the police training camp. Maybe he would introduce you to the instructor. He might give you a few pointers to get you started in the right direction. Our newspaper sponsors the after-school exercise program for young boys and girls."

Dillon stood up and interrupted, "I think we'll talk about an exercise program at our next meeting. If we get a majority vote, I'll go for it. It sounds exciting!"

Joe House rose from his seat, checked his notes, and said, "This question is for the tall boy with the Boy Scout uniform. I'm sorry, I missed your name."

"I'm Garth Waters," Garth spoke up.

"Hello, Garth," the reporter for the Mayfield News said. "Do you enjoy working with the F.B.I. Club?"

"I was so happy when Justin and Pete came over to my house and asked me to join the club," Garth said proudly. "Just like scouting, the F.B.I. members are interested in learning new things and also helping others."

"Can you tell us your goal?" Joe House continued.

"Yes sir, I can," Garth responded. "I want to go to college to study agriculture. My goal is to become a scientist who studies diseases in plants and trees. We lost our entire chestnut crop because of the blight. I want to learn the early signs of diseases in trees and plants so we can find a cure before the entire forest is diseased."

"We need more scientists like that," reporter Joe House stated. "Tell us about your participation in the Boy Scouts."

"Well, I want to make Eagle Scout before I turn sixteen next year. I've learned many useful skills in the Boy Scouts. My scoutmaster Mr. Byrum even helped me build the tree house in my back yard. We used it for our scout troop meetings until Hurricane Hilda uprooted the tree and the tree house was destroyed," Garth replied. "I have earned my Star and Life achievement ranks. Also, I have many of the 21 badges needed for my Eagle rank. I'm a youth group leader at St. James Methodist Church. For my Eagle project, I am helping to build wheelchair ramps at the homes of handicapped people with my grandfather, who belongs to the Golden Kiwanis Club."

"Although you are not yet an Eagle Scout, it appears you are already serving your church and country," the reporter commented.

"Thank you, sir," Garth replied. "I do honestly love my God and our nation."

"This question is for Justin Stewart," Wanda Fish, the reporter from the Mayfield Times remarked. "Didn't I write an article about you and your achievements on the wrestling team, at the local and regional matches?"

"Yes, you did, Ms. Fish," Justin explained. "I went to the state finals and won a silver medal at the matches for my school."

"That is quite an accomplishment for a boy of thirteen," Wanda Fish said, looking at Justin's small frame. "What are your future goals when you graduate from high school?"

"I plan to be a Physical Education teacher. I love sports, especially wrestling," Justin said proudly. "I feel that I can help in the development of strong bodies in young men. My coach has been a great role model for me. Without his help and guidance, I don't think I would have come in second place in the state competition."

"Dillon, this next question is for you," Ms. Betty McNiven said. "Don't you work with your father in his lawn care service?"

"Yes, Ms. McNiven, I sure do," Dillon answered with enthusiasm. "It's hard work, but I want to go to college to study horticulture. My dad just built a greenhouse to grow his own plants for his customers. My dad is a great business manager. I want to be a plant expert. That's an important part of the lawn service too," Dillon explained.

Next, Wanda Fish asked, "Sam, Rick introduced you as Vice President of the F.B.I. Club. Are you interested in the law enforcement field?"

"No," Sam replied, "it's not my main goal. Since I'm tall and enjoy basketball, I would like to be a member of the NBA. Otherwise, I want to be a Medic on the Ambulance squad here in town."

Wanda Fish turned and spoke to everyone in the room. "We are all proud to meet each and every one of you boys. I plan on writing a feature story on the Junior Investigators that will inspire other young people to give unselfishly of their time and talents for their community!"

Police Chief George Adams stepped forward and announced, "Now it's time to present the official award to each of these young men for their bravery, dedication, and resourcefulness on behalf of our great city."

Chief Adams read the commendation aloud to the reporters. "This Commendation is in recognition of bravery, dedication, and resourcefulness on behalf of the City of Mayfield." He held up the certificate. All the members of the City Council had signed it.

Rick spoke up and asked Chief Adams if he could have the floor. "I have an announcement to make."

"Go right ahead, Rick," the chief said as he stepped aside to let Rick have the microphone.

"Before the ceremony began, the members of the F.B.I. Club held an emergency meeting. It was voted unanimously that Joey be allowed to become a member. There is only one condition. Joey will have to stay at the club house when we go on investigations until he is eleven-and-a-half years old. He can handle the communications from there."

Joey jumped up from his chair and said, "I promise not to let you guys down again. I will try to grow up and stay out of trouble."

Jim Murphy of TV station WZAX stepped forward and announced, "I am inviting you boys to be on TV. Because we are a national network news service, your story will be broadcast all over the country. Could you all be at the station about 7:30 tomorrow morning? Betty McNiven, our star interviewer, will meet with you. I'm sure she will want to learn all about your F.B.I. Club. It is so unusual to have such positive news about young people to report."

"We would be proud and honored to appear on your TV station WZAX," Rick replied.

F.B.I. Agent Patterson stepped forward with an announcement, "I am willing to accompany these young men on their TV interview. My senior officer and I also wish to give an Honorary F.B.I. Certificate to each of these young men. Perhaps we might make that presentation during their TV appearance. These boys are setting a high standard for other young boys who want to help their communities. I hope many young people tune in and learn something from these young investigators."

Rick stepped forward and accepted his certificate first. "Thank you very much for this honor," Rick said, as he shook Chief Adams' hand and then the mayor's hand.

"Come on up, Sam, Pete, Dillon, Garth, Joey, and Justin," said the mayor. Each boy received his certificate and shook hands with Chief Adams and the mayor.

Finally, the boys posed for pictures with the mayor and Police Chief George Adams. The boys unrolled and stretched out their clubhouse banner. Each boy held a section in front of him for all to see. The banner displayed the words:

THE F.B.I. CLUB

THE FAMOUS BOY INVESTIGATORS CLUB

Many cameras flashed as the boys smiled from ear to ear with pride in their successful investigations.

Rick said, "Didn't I tell you we'd get a lot of publicity for our efforts? We'll continue our investigations, but for now let's take a break. We can begin our crime watch surveillance again next week."

"We can go out during daylight, right?" Sam asked. "I think it would be safer."

The boys began to laugh with their families and all those in attendance. It was not long before they returned to their club house to make plans for their next adventure.

THE END